SECRETS *of* SCANDALS

SECRETS *of* SCANDALS

JONATHAN HUBERT ADDY

SECRETS OF SCANDALS

ISBN: 97899889023 3 9

Edited by Dr Martin Egblewogbe

Cover Design and Book Layout by
Nene Buer Boyetey
P O Box NM 78, Nima, Accra, Ghana
Email: bigglesmultimedia@gmail.com
Tel: +233 302 333 502 | +233 244 634 204

Published by
DAkpabli & Associates
P O Box 7465, Accra North, Accra, Ghana
Tel: +233 264 339 066 | +233 244 704 250 | +233 247 896 375
Email: info@dakpabli.com

Cover photo is created from photos and sketches by

J.H Addy and painted by Boateng

The photo shows:

James Town Harbour, built in 1872

James Town Fort, built in 1672

James Town Light House, built in 1835 by the Lighterage Company of West Africa

The original hangs on the stairwell of '39 Steps', the residence of the author, at Shiashie, East Legon, Accra

All illustrations in this book were pencil-sketched by the author except the photographs which were extracted from the archives of the historical Accra photographers of Deo Gratias studios of Accra

DEDICATION

To my children

PREFACE

One fine day, I set out to write a story. Many years earlier during my academic life when I was confronted with the task of writing and presenting a thesis to the University of London (after I had collected all my clinical data, perfected and selected photographs and itemised all illustrations, charts and tables, and virtually set out the whole thesis in note form paragraph by paragraph and even chapter by chapter), I suddenly came face-to-face with the actual writing up in prose. Something quite unexpected happened to me at that stage. Inertia descended on me and for several weeks I could not put pen to paper. I seriously advised myself and arrived at two resolutions. Firstly, to write a summary stating clearly the identified problem, the methods to be used to solve them, the anticipated results, the conclusions thereof and the lessons to be learnt. Fortunately, I was able to accomplish the above task in a day. My second profound resolution, which was based on the advice of concerned colleagues (who had experienced the same dilemma but managed to overcome it and produced excellent theses) was to write a few lines, or a paragraph, or a page or even a few pages every blessed day. That tactic worked, for after long painful periods of perseverance I completed writing up in six months and my thesis for MD (old regulation) for the University of London was presented and accepted without interview or viva.

Since the above effort I have written numerous academic original papers, editorials for the Ghana Medical Journal (of which I was the editor for several years) and given many official and informal addresses as President of the Ghana Medical Association using the same method. It was therefore not surprising that I adopted the same method (i.e. writing a few paragraphs each day) in order to complete my first story/novel

Secrets of Scandals, which the reader is about to encounter.

It was after writing the first few pages of the story that I realised that the prose flowed at its best and also very fluently when I pictured the scenes frame by frame in the fashion of creating a motion picture or 'cinema' hence the natural 'birth' of numerous sketches by me which enabled the book to end up illustrated. The first illustration was naturally the map of Gold Coast (1900) which set the scene for the very first paragraph of this book.

The story told in this book is pure fiction; in other words, a figment of my imagination, therefore any reader who detects resemblance to any episode in real life must be assured that the resemblance is entirely coincidental. It must be stated that my love for storytelling was inspired at a very tender age by my grandmother and great grandmother who confessed that they concocted all their stories by recalling what they had gathered from their own late parents who, like themselves, had never been to school and therefore could neither read nor write. I tried to emulate and imitate them, and I am proud to state that my story is devoid of any borrowed material from remote Europe, Asia, Americas, Pacific Oceania et cetera. That my story is purely local and free of foreign adulteration was first noticed by Nana Awere Damoah, the publisher, and Dr Martin Egblewogbe, the editor he engaged to read and assess suitability for publication. Both gentlemen mentioned above, though black and Ghanaian like the author (myself), are a generation younger and belonged not to the South-Eastern ethnic stock of the author.

The editor, a graduate of the University of Ghana and lecturer at same university, with a long experience of editing texts written in English, read the story with great patience. He obviously took detailed notes so that his initial comments revealed several discrepancies. He discussed the contents of the text as though they were real events and the characters as though they really existed. Inconsistencies were pointed out to me and I was obliged to review several details including time frames.

The first meeting or conference with editor and publisher on the text of *Secrets of Scandals* was an eye-opener for me. Hitherto, I had only published scientific papers in Internal Medicine and Dermatology reflecting authentically my postgraduate qualifications and work as consultant physician at Korle Bu Teaching Hospital and University Professor at University of Ghana Medical School for several decades. *Secrets of Scandals* being my first attempt at story writing, I was under the wrong impression that review by editors and referees would not be as demanding as I had experienced regarding scientific papers; but my publisher and editor proved me wrong by confronting me with their detailed unfavourable review of my text and further stated without mincing words that if I earnestly wanted to publish a 'NOVEL' I must be prepared to work hard for it.

After overcoming my initial shock, I resolved to take on the challenge they had proposed. I corrected all my mistakes and commented on and explained all that they found odd because they were not familiar with the customs and some of the cultural norms of the principal characters in the story.

The story was set in Accra (a coastal fairly large early 20th century township at the south-east corner of the then Gold Coast) and its environs along the coast all the way to Sekondi, situated in the south-west as shown on the map opposite page and the adjoining deep forest hinterland parallel and a few miles north of the Accra to Sekondi coastline described above. Both my grand and great grandmother who told us numerous longwinded stories by the lantern side from after supper to bedtime were Ga-Dangbes from South-Eastern Gold Coast

Colony who had not experienced formal education, which in those years was organised by European missionaries for whom the Bible was the only legitimate or appropriate reading material for 'natives'. Therefore, our elders told us stories well and truly native and devoid of foreign influences and in this my very first attempt at storytelling I resolved to do same. I knew I had achieved my wish when the editor and publisher were utterly shocked by the total unfamiliarity with the culture, habits and well-established ceremonies of the characters in the book.

The first two problems the editor and publisher identified concerned 'non-English' words used frequently by the characters during conversation, and secondly the non-European but rather typical local expressions of ideas. I convinced them I had difficulty in finding the exact English words appropriate for the spirit of the narrative hence the use the more accurate Ga word or phrase every now and then, and that a glossary needed to be created for the benefit of all readers. As regards the second problem, I confessed that all my original thoughts, ideas and narratives are in my mother tongue which is obviously Ga, which is then translated into English which in our age is recognised by all and sundry as the language of all people. Indeed, the editor asked me to state the language of the conversation among the characters; the characters spoke English as shown in the text, obviously not classical or idiomatic as spoken by the owners of that language. I am aware that my English has many faults and make no claim to producing English Literature. All I have attempted to do is to produce Literature in English.

In order to further explain the statement at the end of the last paragraph, I need to refer to an important question the editor asked on several occasions. He wanted to know who was talking to who, as the rules he was used to had not been strictly adhered to. My immediate response was that

Secrets of Scandals is not a novel in the English or European tradition; in other words, it is not English Literature but rather *Literature in English* as conceptualised not so long ago when storytellers of Nigeria like Chinua Achebe, and of Ghana like Ayi Kwei Armah burst on the literary scene. They earnestly wrote their stories and even at the Nobel Prize level were challenged by prejudiced stereotyped Western authors that they did not adhere to the established rules. They successfully defended themselves by insisting that theirs were pieces of literature in English and not English literature.

I set out to tell a story with the aim of exposing to future readers the mannerisms, ceremonies and peculiar habits of a proud and enlightened people, especially as to how they solved their problems. On careful reading of the story, one would find an elder invariably trying to teach the younger ones the culture, traditions and principles of natural science underlying their most intricate practices. The reader must try and identify the teaching sessions which are numerous and scattered through the whole length of the story.

The original sub-title *A Novel by J.H. Addy* became problematic after the first conference with the referees/reviewers. I realised that this humble piece of writing is not a novel in the traditional English Literature model or style. It is a simple story told by a native of Gold Coast Colony (now Ghana).

What appears on the cover is appropriate.

PROLOGUE

In the year 1900, Eric Wuta was living in Sekondi and working at the harbour as a shipping agent and a merchant. It was his well-established habit to visit the family in Accra several times a year. On one such visit he had an illicit union (which resulted in a pregnancy) with Robyn Quinton-Taki, the daughter of his late uncle Jeff who was the elder brother of James Quinton-Taki, and in whose house Robyn resided and worked as a house help. Robyn was the biological daughter of Jeff who had died six months earlier when Robyn was sixteen. Robyn knew her father well and remembered the circumstances which compelled her own mother to leave him. After her father's death she was adopted by her kind uncle James Quinton-Taki. James, the famous Accra lawyer, had twin sons and a daughter, and insisted on school and college education for all of them. However, Robyn was made to stay at home doing house-hold chores.

The Quinton-Taki family was shattered by the anticipation of the public outcry and gossip, the natural consequence of news of the pregnancy becoming public. However, Eric and Robyn hid their relationship and the pregnancy so well that by the time the household and the patriarch Quinton-Taki himself got wind of it, it was too late as Robyn was already four months pregnant and an intervention was not an option.

A baby girl was thus born to Eric and Robyn on 1st August 1901 and named Martha. In order to prevent the new-born baby becoming fatherless or nameless according to Ga custom, young Eric Wuta was obliged to outdoor and name the baby exactly one week after her birth. The customary proceedings were insisted on by the new baby's double grand uncle notwithstanding the fact that Eric Wuta was already married by ordinance to Mrs. Elsa Efua Wuta (nee Coleman) of Cape Coast, and the couple Mr. and Mrs. Eric Wuta belonged to the high society scene of Sekondi-Takoradi. Eric and Elsa had been married for only three years prior and had been blessed with a son two years before the birth of Martha. Eric Wuta and his extended family in Accra managed to keep his wife in the dark for a short time, until the news broke in Sekondi and Eric's hitherto devoted and kind wife got wind of it and all hell broke loose.

CHAPTER ONE

SEKONDI

The year was AD 1900, and the place was Sekondi in the Gold Coast, a coastal town 150 miles, west of Accra as the crow flies. Further west the coastal road continued for another 50 miles to Half Assini at the farthest South-Western corner of the Gold Coast. The young Eric Wuta had re-located here in 1898 from his hometown Accra to further his career as a shipping agent. He had left his well-to-do family behind in frustration and anger, having wanted to go to England to study law. His family refused to sponsor him because they were quite satisfied with their current family lawyer in the person of Eric's uncle James Quinton-Taki, son of the legendary Gold Coast merchant and tycoon Stonewall Quinton-Taki. At that time there were no government scholarships and families had to pool funds in order to send their bright young ones to Europe to do law, medicine, engineering or the arts in order to work on their own or better still enter the colonial civil service with "European" posts. Had he opted to do medicine, perhaps the family would have sponsored him, but to insist on doing law was to challenge his uncle James and that was unacceptable. Having failed to persuade his family, he settled for the next best thing and that was to follow the footsteps of his famous maternal grandfather, Stonewall Quinton-Taki, into business. Armed with the famous Quinton-Taki recommendation he joined a shipping firm at the Accra port. It did not take long for the bright young man to show his mettle. Stonewall was quick to appreciate Eric's aptitude for that kind of business and wisely advised him to re-locate to Sekondi in order to establish his own business, which subsequently became the first entirely African owned shipping organization at Sekondi Port. Within

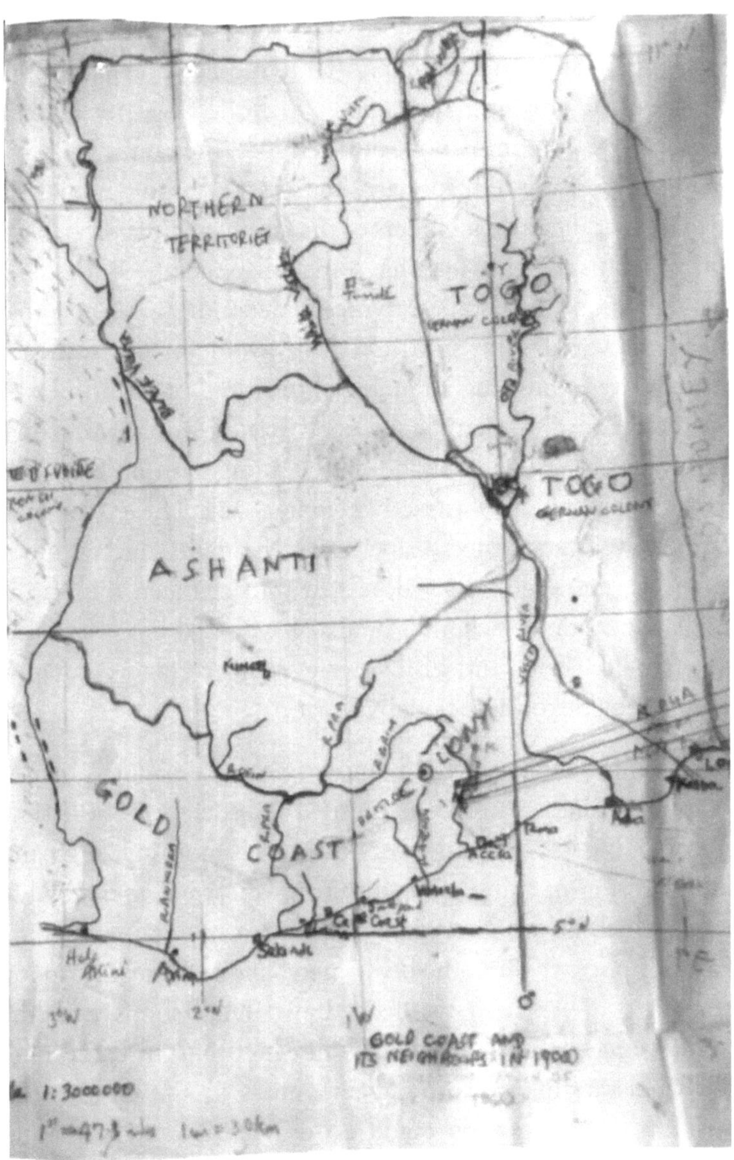

Gold Coast Colony and its Neighbours in 1900

one short year his establishment in Sekondi became rich and famous. Eric became a very busy and successful merchant and hardly spent any time at home. After living all alone in Sekondi for about a year, and now aged 25, he felt the need for a constant female companion. Furthermore, the family in Accra had been advising him to marry for several reasons. In view of the fact that the male members of the family had the propensity for womanising and hearing some unspeakable stories and scandals about their son's activities in Sekondi, they knew that marriage would calm him and help avoid further scandals. Sekondi was a bustling commercial town full of beautiful well educated Fante women from Cape Coast, Elmina, Komenda, Tarkwa, Takoradi and Sekondi itself. Young dashing Eric soon ran into one of these attractive women called Elsie Coleman from a well-established Cape Coast family. Courtship was intensive, marriage followed, and within eighteen months of Eric's relocation at Sekondi, he had a wife and baby son. The two families (Eric's and Elsie's) were overjoyed, and the happy couple took Sekondi society by storm.

Despite his new marital and family status, Eric Wuta pursued a typical businessman tycoon lifestyle and spent very little time at home. He left the house very early each morning to go and supervise the opening and setting up of several merchandise shops which he ran in town. Apart from a warehouse near the Sekondi port where he held his merchandise from Liverpool, Hamburg or Amsterdam, he had two retail shops near the Market circle. He was able to maximise his profits by combining the wholesale business and retail outlets to the envy of his business colleagues who could do only either and not both. Thus, he created a large number of enemies and rivals, but his buoyant personality and his closeness to several European merchant friends and powerful government officials whom he bribed freely and frequently enabled him to thrive and prosper despite the persistent scheming of conspirators aimed at his downfall. The real price he had to pay for his success in the business sector was that his household continued to suffer from neglect and several disasters befell him in the course of time. The first major disaster occurred in his hometown Accra which he was obliged to visit often when family matters came up. On one such visit to Accra he encountered a new face in the household.

The year was 1900 and it was January, and the beginning of a brand-new century. The ship *M.V. Densu* of Elder Dempster Lines had reached Accra Port early in the morning. After disembarkation, he hired a horse-drawn carriage. His suitcase and a few other belongings were loaded on the carriage and the driver asked,

"Where to on this bright fine morning?"

Eric answered, "Take me to lawyer Quintin-Taki's mansion."

The house was on the outskirts of town, at Tudu, not far from the Government Well at Kinbu.

The driver was an expert who knew the town of Accra very well. He manoeuvred the vehicle with dexterity from the lighthouse junction through the broad lane now named High Street. They rolled along for about a mile through the densely populated central Accra also known as Kinka We or Dutch Accra or Usher Town

They passed Ussher Fort, built by the Dutch to rival James fort of the English. And continued eastwards to Atukpai where they turned north onto Lutterodt street. Veering through Pagan road, they sped northwards and soon they were at Kinbu junction from where he could see his uncle's beautiful white mansion. On reaching the gate they opened it and the carriage

Eric on his way to Q-T at Q-T Mansions from the port of Accra

rolled along the tree-lined gravel road noisily to the entrance of the main building. The noise had alerted the household and standing at the main heavy odum door was an elegant tall slim girl wearing the simple clothing of a housemaid. He was impressed by the dignified good manners of the maidservant and he tried to engage her in conversation or an interrogation as to her background. The girl was reticent, in obedience to the strict instructions she had received from Mrs. Quintin-Taki as regards her behaviour to unknown visitors to the house. The rule which she carefully memorised stated clearly that on no account should she answer any questions put by strangers who came calling at the gate except to ask that they kindly wait while she went to notify the elders of the household, or that the elders were out, and she was only allowed to take a message. If the visitor insisted on waiting, then they would be seated on the breezy porch in front of the house and offered a drink of cool water.

What baffled the young girl at the door was that this visitor behaved differently from all previous ones. Not only did he appear to know the house well, he also somehow knew the habits of the elderly inmates. He was aware that at that time of the day papa lawyer would be at work but was sure that the madam of the house should be at home. He was also aware that the children would all be at school. At first the visitor ignored her and shouted for the missus, but when he got no answer, he turned to Robyn who then informed him that Madam went out in the morning. Eric then decided to pay attention to this maid who seemed to be in perfect control of the situation.

Eric was offered a comfortable cane chair on the porch as the pleasant morning breeze from the south caressed his face and rustled the foliage of the tall trees in the garden. The maid put his suitcase in the hall and came back to offer him the cold

Robyn at the front door of Q-T mansions

drinking water of traditional welcome. He drank the water and politely thanked the maid who was surprised that this fine gentleman was quite different from other uppity visitors who looked down on her and treated her with contempt. She naturally warmed up to this new visitor whose name she did not yet know and dared not ask.

Eric sat and waited for about an hour and then he heard the rattling noise of an approaching carriage towards the entrance porch of the mansion. He sat up eagerly hoping to see who was in the cart before he was seen. When the cart pulled up, the driver jumped out of his driving seat and went to the back of the carriage to open the door and help Mrs. Quinton-Taki down. When she saw the visitor she shouted, "Eric, welcome home. I knew you were coming but I did not expect you so soon. We were expecting the Takoradi boat to arrive at 12 noon."

"It was a very speedy passage. Indeed, we had hardly recovered from the usual night reveries on the deck when we were informed that we were within sight of Accra port. We disembarked at 9.00 am and I got here at 10.00. Your efficient new maid informed me that you were out after I had made a fool of myself ignoring her and shouting frantically, for I was sure that at ten you must be at home."

"I left the house even before your uncle left for work because I needed to attend a kpodziemɔ for a baby boy of a young cousin at the Asere quarter. How are you? Did Robyn give you breakfast?"

Eric asked, "Who is Robyn?"

Mrs. Quinton-Taki was surprised by the question. "Have you forgotten that we sent you word about 3 months ago that your uncle Jeff had died at Pakro and her only daughter Robyn

"Atuu" Eric and Mrs Q-T greet each other on the porch

had come to live with us in Accra? You did not even write to offer your condolences. Robyn is your first cousin by English custom, but according to our custom you and Robyn are *nun bi ke yoo bi.*

"I am very sorry I did not respond appropriately to that letter. I will apologise to my uncle as soon as he comes home. I will also apologise to my cousin Robyn even now on two counts: first for failing to write to express my condolences at the time of her bereavement, and secondly for not regarding her as a close relative deserves but rather as a maidservant. I hope that my apologies will be accepted."

"Oh! Eric, there is no need to be upset."

"Aunt Karen, by accepting my apologies you have automatically given me permission to ask a question."

"Please go ahead."

"How old is Robyn?"

"She is 17."

"Is it because my cousin is too old that she is not at school with the other children?"

"Your uncle is the right person to answer this question. He decided to adopt Robyn and I agreed wholeheartedly with the idea. All the customary rites of adoption have been performed and your uncle is the legitimate father of your cousin Robyn Quinton-Taki. When the problem first came up and you were summoned to the family meeting for discussion you refused to come. Please wait for your uncle, he has strong views on our new daughter and the manner in which she must be brought up."

"Sure, I will discuss the problem with my uncle, it is never too late to mend. It is not fair to treat Robyn as an orphan or a miserable villager and maidservant. She has rights and things must be done correctly."

Eric then asked Mrs. Quinton-Taki when she expected her husband home for lunch.

"Don't disturb him at lunch time…remember your uncle is getting on in years, he will be 50 next month. If he were in the village, he would be whiling away the time peacefully as an old man while his younger relatives toiled in the farms for his benefit. Here in Accra, he is at the peak of his professional working life and expected to put in long hours. He has only 2 hours to have lunch and siesta before he goes back to the office at Victoriaborg to consult with clients and colleagues. He will come back at 7.00 pm in a more relaxed mood; I suggest you talk to him after dinner."

Eric appreciated the wisdom of his aunt's point of view and decided to postpone all family discussions to dinner time that same evening.

THE DISCUSSION BETWEEN ERIC AND HIS UNCLE

Papa Lawyer or QT to family and friends, arrived home at 2.00 pm instead of the expected 1.30 pm. His wife was on the veranda to meet him with a warm greeting and a quick hug. "You are 30 minutes late," she remarked.

"Yes my dear, I am sorry, the judge went on and on with the reading of the judgement which luckily went in my client's favour…lucky because it was quite close and I really appreciated his effort because he had to delve deep into the archives to come out with a first-class judgement."

"Heii! Papa Lawyer, just because it went in your favour you are in a good mood and the judge did well. I shudder to imagine what mood you would have been in had the case gone the other way."

"It could not have gone the other way. I put a lot of effort into it."

"I hope your client will appreciate your toil and reward you well."

"The client has already done both; dear wife let me tell you a secret, with the proceeds of this case alone we can build a second house bigger than this one."

"Where is Robyn?" he asked, raising his voice.

"Papa I am coming,"

"Oh! There you are, tell Abotsi to bring me a cold bottle of Beck's and a glass,"

At that moment he saw Eric coming out of the study. He therefore told Robyn,

"Let Abotsi bring two beers instead, I will have a drink with Eric on the veranda. Eric you are welcome, when did you arrive?"

"I arrived at 9.00 am."

"You have delayed your trip to Accra by 6 months and a lot has happened in those 6 months. Your uncle Jeff died as you were informed. He has since been buried according to custom, audit has been done and important decisions taken and executed all on your blind side. For example, his daughter has been adopted by me and she now lives with us in this house. We will talk more about that at dinner time…right now I am tired and I must have lunch and a short siesta before my afternoon session in my office in town."

The two gentlemen, one a successful Accra lawyer and the other an up-and-coming Sekondi merchant, uncle and nephew respectively, sat on the breezy veranda and enjoyed a cold beer. Meanwhile Robyn had set the table for lunch and the two gentlemen and Mrs Quintin-Taki soon sat down for cocoyam fufu and tasty goat head light soup. Eric noticed that Robyn was around the kitchen and in the backyard with the other servants and was not allowed near the table. He decided to talk about this at dinner, when his uncle's own children would be around.

The meal was good and utterly filling and Eric also enjoyed the tatale which being a Ga invention was not part of the culinary delights of Sekondi. Papa Lawyer felt drowsy after the heavy meal but complied with accepted practice and walked up and down the long veranda a few times to allow the food to settle down well. He then went to his bedroom to lie down and enjoy his afternoon siesta. He slept for about 80 minutes, got up and hurriedly washed his face with soap and water, dressed up in a light weight tropicalised light grey suit, put on his felt hat and called his driver to take him to his office at law chambers at Victoriaborg.

He only worked intensively for 90 minutes in the office and he was done. He had managed to interview two important clients from whom his clerk had collected all the relevant facts of the case and the exorbitant consultation fee which was far above the average charged by other top lawyers in Accra. It was time to rush home to attend to pressing domestic affairs, therefore he was not able to hang around with his colleagues for the usual socials. The drive home took 20 minutes. It was exactly 6.30 pm when he entered the hall where his wife and nephew Eric were already seated in anticipation of the family discussion.

Family meeting before dinner. From Left to Right: Lawyer James, Mrs. Q-T and Mr Eric Wuta

Lawyer Q-T started the discussion as skilfully as only he could by remarking thus: “Let us do this delicate business now and before dinner as our children will be joining us for dinner.”

Eric immediately asked, “Which children exactly will be joining us?”

Q-T immediately recognised that he had blundered and played into the hands of his nephew. He quickly decided on a direct and truthful way out: he therefore mentioned the names of his 3 children, Kate and the twin boys Bob and Billy, also known as Robert and William. Mrs Quintin-Taki quickly understood the clever move Eric had made by asking which children will be joining us for dinner. Eric saw his advantage and pressed on by asking the obvious questions.

“What about myself and Robyn, are we also your children?”

Papa Lawyer retorted, “Of course you Eric will be joining us at table, but certainly not Robyn.”

“Why?” asked Eric.

Q-T looked briefly at his wife then at Eric, and said, “Ask her.”

His wife did not wait for the question but rather asked permission to speak. When permission was granted, she said, “My dear husband and my dear son, I am grateful for this opportunity to speak. In all humility let me state that throughout our long – 15 years to be exact – years of marriage, we have had our differences. I know I am opinionated, but I am happy to say that my husband is strong, forthright and equally opinionated. We have argued on several important and trivial issues, but they have always been in secret and no matter how divergent our views were, we have always managed to arrive at a consensus to present with a united front. My husband and I had long discussions on the issues and in the end, we came to a consensus which we presented to the family in public. My husband being the head of the family is also the spokesman who presented our agreed conclusions and I think he should present our views to you."

Q-T agreed to do the presentation as follows: "When your uncle and my elder brother Jeffery died and was buried, urgent problems long anticipated but not thoroughly contemplated caught up with us and we had to act fast. When I say we I mean the extended family of which I am currently the head. Let me start with a bit of history. Your grandfather and my father, the late grand old man of blessed memory was born in 1825. He was one of the great merchants of Accra who did business with the Europeans who traded along our shores. Stonewall Kwatelai Quintin-Taki married early at 24 and produced his first born in 1850 in the person of your mother Catherine. The next was Jeff my elder brother who was born in 1852. I was the third, born in 1856 and your aunt the last of Stonewall's children was born in 1860. Jeff moved into the hinterland because he was keen on farming and there spent his whole working life growing cash crops successfully on our family land between Mangoase and Pakro. He married a local woman and was blessed with one daughter, Robyn, who is the subject of our discussion this evening. Your uncle Jeff was stubborn and hence a difficult man to live with. Several years ago, we heard the news from third parties that Jeff's wife had absconded and gone and married a local farmer with whom she eventually produced several sons and daughters and never bothered to visit Jeff's daughter whom she had so atrociously abandoned when she was only 6 years old. Your proud uncle single-handedly looked after the motherless girl till he died leaving her as a 16-year-old orphan amongst strangers on a lonely farm. He made a will in which he stated that all his worldly belongings including his farms should be looked after by the family with me as head and with

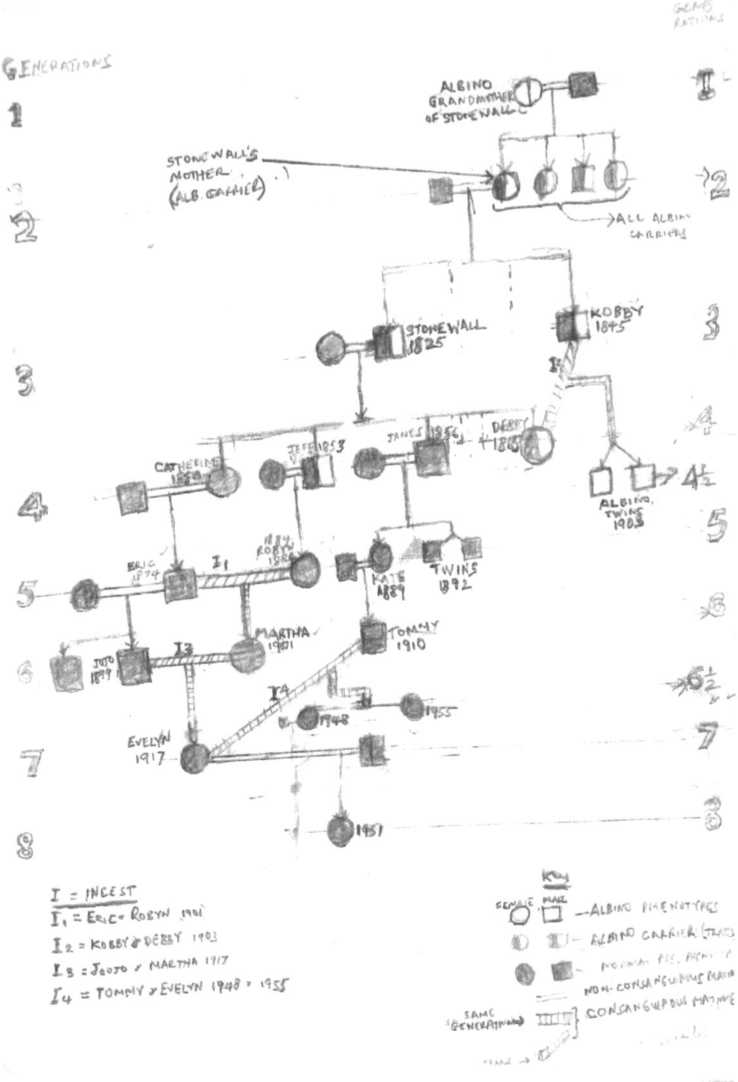

GENERATIONS
ALBINO GRANDMOTHER OF STONEWALL
STONEWALL'S MOTHER (ALB. CARRIER)
ALL ALBINO CARRIERS
STONEWALL 1825
KOBBY 1845
CATHERINE
JEFF 1853
JAMES 1856
DEBBY
ALBINO TWINS 1903
ERIC 1874
ROBYN
KATE 1889
TWINS 1892
MARTHA 1901
TOMMY 1910
JOJO 1899
EVELYN 1917
1948
1955
1951
I = INCEST
I1 = ERIC & ROBYN 1901
I2 = KOBBY & DEBBY 1903
I3 = JOOJO & MARTHA 1917
I4 = TOMMY & EVELYN 1948 & 1955
KEY
FEMALE
MALE
ALBINO PHENOTYPES
ALBINO CARRIER (TRAITS)
NON-CONSANGUINEOUS MATING
CONSANGUINEOUS MATING
SAME GENERATION

Family tree

the condition they will all be transferred to his daughter Robyn when she attained the age of 21 or when she got married and produced her own children and grandchildren to whom he bequeathed his bona fide legacy from generation to generation.

"The family in its wisdom decided that your late uncle's wishes must be followed, otherwise a dangerous precedent would be started which would put all and sundry in fear that our wishes would not be held sacred. The family consensus was that Robyn was to relocate to my house and be looked after as though she were my own daughter. I had no objection. Robyn moved into this house 3 weeks after her father's death and she has stayed here peacefully for the past 6 months. She has fitted into her new environment gracefully and I am happy to say that she gets on very well with my wife. She is hard working, and my wife will bear witness that she virtually supervises the two housemaids currently working in this house. She has her own room in the outhouse and my wife has helped her to furnish it to a respectable standard."

Eric then cut in.

"Uncle I have two questions, first question, if the family decided that she should stay here with the status of a daughter, why is she living in the outhouse with the maids and houseboys while your children who are her siblings are living and sleeping in the main house? Or to put it in another way why is she not living in the main house where she rightfully belongs? My second question is the more difficult one and I have to couch it carefully so that it does sound offensive: I mean well, I do not want to create turmoil and distress. Although at 17 she is too old to start formal schooling, bearing in mind the tradition in this family that all must go to school and learn something, why is Robyn not at school like your children? I am aware that she is 17, but she seems smart and intelligent and I am sure she would benefit from a vocational education coupled with night school at least to learn how to read and write. Surely there is no age limit as far as education is concerned?"

Q-T responded briskly. "Eric, when we summoned you to the family meeting at which these matters were discussed you refused to come."

"Uncle I was busy; besides I have confidence in you. I knew you would take the right decisions."

"No! It was a big gathering and your mother and I were the only ones on Robyn's side. The idea that she would inherit the whole estate of her late father was a difficult pill to swallow for the majority of family members and the pressure on us to sell Jeff's estate and share the proceeds was great. Having secured that part of the will the question of her education was shelved for the sake of peace."

"Uncle the girl now lives with you, and nobody has the right to block her education or reduce her status to that of a maidservant in this house except you."

"Eric please bear in mind that I live here with a wife and 3 children, they also have rights, privileges and emotions which you should weigh against the current situation. I am sure your aunt has something to say. Marian, you have the floor, please say something to our nephew."

"Eric, the dialogue with your uncle on this subject has been ongoing for the past six months and the reason why your uncle has requested me at this stage to say something is because the last time we spoke, I came out with a proposition which he accepted. We are in the process of implementing it. It is as follows: having both observed how well our 3 children get on with Robyn, and how genuinely fond Robyn is of them, we spoke to them, that is our children, and they affirmed that they would be happy to share with their cousin. Indeed, our daughter is yearning to share her room with her for companionship just as the twin boys also share a room. We dilly-dallied while we tried to come to terms with the change and you have provided the final push to enable us to effect the change from tomorrow."

"My dear wife you have spoken well and I thank you. I will not allow our nephew Eric to embarrass us any further, the change will take place now and it is going to be symbolised by Robyn joining us at table for dinner."

"Uncle," Eric said, "you have taken the wind out of my sails, and I have nothing more to say."

"Let us go to dinner," Papa Lawyer announced in his loud baritone voice. This gave the signal for Robyn and the maids in the kitchen to bring the food to the table. On arrival at the dining table Papa Lawyer did a quick calculation in his head and asked Robyn to set two more places at table. The first was for Mrs Wuta, and the second, he added, was for Robyn who would also be joining them at table for dinner henceforth. He then advised Robyn to go and get into formal clothes to match her three cousins who would be there soon and all dressed up.

Robyn went quickly to her room and changed into her nice outing frock and a pair of shoes, bearing in mind what her young cousin Kate was wearing when she last saw her. When they got to the dining table, they all stood still awaiting instructions as to where to sit. Papa Lawyer had anticipated the situation and had already worked everything out. He asked his wife to take her usual place to the right of the table head where he himself usually sat. Opposite Mrs Q-T was the place reserved for her eldest daughter Kate except when Eric was visiting when he sat to the immediate left of Papa Lawyer and

Extended family at dinner

displaced Kate one step down, but on this occasion that place having been restored to Kate, Eric was moved to the farther table head opposite the major table head which was occupied by traditional head of household. To the right of Eric he placed Mrs Wuta Eric's mother and to Eric's left he placed Robyn. The twin boys were then placed opposite each other in the middle, i.e., Robert between Mrs Q-T and Robyn and William between Kate and Mrs Wuta popularly known to the children as auntie Catherine who arrived just in time for the dinner. She took her place to the right of her son opposite her niece Robyn. She noticed the changes and decided to keep quiet about them and say nothing until after dinner. On this occasion the master of the house himself decided to say the prayers before dinner. "Bow down your heads for prayers. Dear Lord and master of this house, we thank you for this evening and this family. May the peace which you have bestowed on us this evening remain with us forever; bless this food, and while we eat to replenish our energy and spirits, make us mindful of the needs of others in the name of Jesus Christ your own begotten son. Amen."

The meal that evening consisted of grilled cured tilapia garnished with onion, tomatoes, various local exotic peppers in an omelette, a tasty dish of the Ga people. It was served with aboloo, cooked yam, and sweet potatoes. The men washed the food down with cold beer while the women and children drank lemonade. Papa Lawyer was about to say grace after meals when his sister stopped him and said, "I brought desert."

That was the signal for her maid Ashami who was waiting for this moment near the kitchen door to walk in with the delicious nutmeg and cinnamon flavoured pancakes for all to enjoy. Grace after meal was said by Mrs Wuta after which Papa Lawyer remarked that he had enjoyed the whole evening and he regretted that it was not a Saturday or even a Friday but rather a Wednesday which meant that the morrow was a full working day and a poor practising lawyer like him unlike those on holiday like Eric who could continue the party with more pancakes and tots of brandy while he retired to go and rest.

As soon as lawyer Q-T walked out, the stiff formal atmosphere disappeared and the noise level doubled. Eric's mother took over with her usual funny jokes and stories. She was now free to comment on the conspicuous changes she had observed on arrival. She looked at Mrs. Q-T and nodded. That was her way of politely asking her permission to speak. Mrs Q-T nodded back which meant permission had been granted and remarked, "Robyn, your well-deserved new status pleases my heart and I thank God and you all. I sensed the happiness especially that of the head of the house and his lovely wife my sister-in-law. As for the children they have shared their secrets with me and I know exactly how they feel. I must leave now and go to my own house perfectly happy that my brother's home is full of joy."

The following morning the servants at the outhouse were the first get to out of bed awakened as usual by background hum of human activity from the nearby Zongo and the call to worship from the tower of the Mosque. The servants rushed to the household well and drew several buckets of water. Papa Lawyer preferred to bathe with cold water a practice from his youthful days which he had vowed to continue despite pleadings from his dear wife who preferred warm or almost hot water baths. After bathing and dressing Mr and Mrs Q-T had a quick breakfast and left the house in quick succession, Q-T at 7.30 am because he had to brush up a few things before he appeared before the Chief Justice whom he was scheduled to address in a high-profile case. The missus had to attend a family meeting at Asere and she left home at 7.45 am. When Eric leisurely woke up at 8.30 am he realised that both his uncle and his wife were out. The servants were obliged to provide him with water for bathing and were not surprised when Eric confirmed that he preferred very cold baths for its invigorating effect. After the bath he dressed up casually and went and sat on the veranda to continue his holiday away from the business worries of Sekondi. For a brief moment he missed his wife and his one-year-old son Erico but he quickly brushed that away knowing very well that his Sekondi household was full of visitors namely his in-laws and some of their local relatives and friends. He preferred to spend the morning thinking about the events of the previous evening, especially Robyn who was now happily relocated in the main house where she rightly belonged. The joy which he felt in his bosom when he thought about Robyn was alarming because it transcended what was expected between cousins. It felt more like an infatuation if not love itself. At 26, he was still youthful and he had had similar inappropriate crushes before but they were short-lived and soon fizzled out without consummation. He was therefore sure this one would be the same. He heard approaching footsteps and was relieved that they were those of the elderly chief housekeeper who had only come to enquire what he would like for breakfast.

After breakfast Eric returned to the airy veranda to read a Sherlock Holmes novel. The heavy breakfast combined with the morning breeze lulled his senses and he dozed off. It was not a deep sleep; indeed he was serially awakened by the chief housekeeper and her young maid on their way to market, then by the groundsman on an errand, and lastly by the cook on his way to the butcher's shop at Zongo. He did a quick calculation by elimination and he realised that only two people were still in the house namely himself and his beautiful cousin Robyn. He felt an irresistible urge to go looking for her, if at least to be assured that she was not lonely or in distress. Curiosity as to what she was up to all alone in her room got the better part of him, so he plucked courage and climbed the stairs. On reaching the landing he instinctively looked round and all was indeed quiet. He turned into the corridor leading to the girls' room. The door was shut, he listened carefully for a sound but he was confronted with absolute silence. The possibility that she had sneaked out of the house on his blind side almost frightened and disappointed him, and in his utter state of bewilderment he pushed open the door without knocking. To his utter amazement he was confronted with a scene which was an erotic pleasure to behold. Robyn had just come out from the bath and was standing entirely naked from head to toe in order to do her powdering and oiling prior to dressing up. She was facing the window next to a full-length mirror so he was privileged to see both frontal and rear nudity of this tall, slim shapely, elegant womanhood truly in her prime with perfect proportions including the appropriate protrusions only the healthy young black woman could be endowed with. He was about to crawl into his shell by retreating across the open door when she said, "come in!" nonchalantly.

He replied, "Sorry to intrude on your privacy without knocking."

Robyn then replied without hesitation, "Apologies accepted." In the interim she had covered her nakedness with a neat wrapper and had turned to face him squarely across the full breadth of the medium-sized girls' bedroom. He looked at her in the eye and she stared back without any coyness which action convinced him that she expected him to come looking for her sooner or later. Eric then recovered his composure and said, "I will wait for you on the veranda because whatever I wanted to see you for can wait."

Eric encounters Robyn after her bath. facing full length mirror in her room

To which Robyn replied, “That is a loaded statement, nevertheless I will come to the veranda as soon I finish dressing up.” Eric returned to the breezy veranda, sat down, shut his eyes as if in a daydream and waited for his cousin rather anxiously with pounding heart and sweating palms.

She finally arrived and stood for a split second only because being a perfect gentleman Eric asked her to sit down without any delay. She did so with confidence, knowing that she belonged to the household and the process whereby the change was effected had been championed by this very nice gentleman who was her own bona fide cousin. She decided to take the initiative and break the ice of the mutually desired encounter by thanking him for last night and proceeded as follows:

“Cousin Mr Eric Wuta, thank you very much for your interventions which have led to a most respectable status for an otherwise and hitherto poor uneducated village girl.”

Eric now fully relaxed was amazed by the inherent wisdom and wit of his young cousin. He naturally assumed the typical Sekondi type jovial mood and met her cousin wit for wit by continuing the conversation thus:

“First of all, you need not address me in that severe formal manner, I am your very close blood relation, first cousins by European terminology or ‘nunbi ke yoobi’, you being the ‘nunbi’ or male sibling’s child and me the female sibling’s child. The definition is very important for the elders because whereas a yoobi nu can marry a nunbi yoo the reverse is not allowed for reasons you can work out yourself or I will explain later. Secondly, I am only 10 years and a few months older than you therefore you are at liberty and indeed it is your inherent birth right to treat me as your co-equal and call me by my real name Eric or brother Nii Kwartei as all my other cousins do. Thirdly although I accept your thanks for your new status, you must remember that the master of the household Lawyer Quintin-Taki our uncle and his good wife made that good decision, I was a mere catalyst."

"Well cousin Eric you have spoken well and I am proud of you. You have acted as an elder brother and a peace maker, but I can assure you that I know far more than you will ever know as regards my status in this house. Remember that I had lived in this house for 6 months before you appeared on the scene and I have been through a lot which for the sake of peace you should never know. From what I have gathered about your nature so far I am quite confident that this our current conversation would never leak, because my uncle and his wife must never know that it happened. Suffice it to say that I know exactly the part you played and I swear I will be forever grateful to you. My uncle and his wife are very good people. I like them very much and am aware the family pressures they have endured in their efforts to ensure that my father's wishes on my inheritance were complied with. The current status change is a bonus; a true testimony of their good nature and genuine humanity."

It was Eric's turn to speak and he decided to change the subject because he had a lot to say and plan. Time was far spent, soon the house would start filling up with inmates returning from various errands.

"Robyn, you are a very intelligent well-spoken young woman at 17, what happened to your education? Why did your father not send you to school?"

"My father is dead, and I cannot pretend to be able to tell you his mind, but I can certainly tell you my own story. There were schools around the farm, but the distances were great. The nearest school was a good 2 hours walk from the farmstead along a lonely footpath deep in the forest. Despite the distance when I was 8 years old my father enrolled me and took me to school each morning and a good Samaritan teacher arranged for people to bring me back home after school. You must remember that my mother quit the farmstead when I was 6 years old. She moved out of the neighbourhood and we never saw her again, rumours were that she re-married and travelled to another country. Attending school daily proved impossible under my circumstances, bearing in mind that my father depended on me at the tender age of 9 for all the housework in addition to preparing meals so that he could concentrate on his farming. It came as no surprise when he decided that I should quit regular school and attend Sunday school only from 3.00 pm to 5.00 pm. He personally took me to the Sunday school in the Methodist church of the same town where I had attended regular school, hung around until school was over and then walked back home with me. This went on regularly for 4 years when his illness set in, and thus my schooling was truncated. At Sunday school it was strictly vernacular studies. We were taught the Ga alphabet and how to read Ga so that we could read the Ga Bible. The attention on writing was half-hearted, nonetheless we tried and those of who were capable and keen managed to learn how to write a few sentences in Ga. That I can read and write in Ga is a secret I have kept away from this household, but I am prepared to share that secret with you so that when you are away from here we can exchange letters in Ga. I trust you can condescend to reply my Ga letters in Ga."

Eric was flabbergasted by her thoughts and he showed it by wanting to know to what address he should write and lo and behold she had a readymade answer.

"The letter can be addressed to me and marked for collection at the James Town Post Office, at regular intervals I would go there and ask the postmaster for any letters addressed to Robyn Quintin-Taki for collection. I trust you like writing and would endeavour to reply all my letters promptly."

"I like writing and I assure you that all your letters will be replied promptly".

To which she replied, "Thanks be to God for good writers!" and they both laughed heartily.

Humour is a great catalyst for the development of affection and love and they knew that this bond starting with so much humour and wit this morning was going to last for a long time. Eric then announced that he had finished whatever he came to do in Accra, and he would be on the early morning Elder Dempster steamship the following day. The grandfather clock in the lounge struck 11, which meant that inmates of the house who had gone on various errands would be back soon and this pleasant meeting had to come to an abrupt end. Eric was in a very happy mood and asked Robyn to bring him a bottle of beer. Robyn was to serve herself some lemonade and not beer which was alcoholic and reserved for adults of 21 and above. Robyn complied and brought him a beer from the ice chest and she retired to the kitchen to wait for the kitchen staff in order to help them with the cooking.

The cook Mami Ashami and her assistant young Tetele rushed in through the gate at 11.15 am and hurriedly entered the kitchen by the back door and started preparing lunch. At about 12 noon Mrs Q-T arrived in the carriage at the front door driven by Ataa Kwami who jumped from the driver's seat, came round to open the door and helped the middle-aged slightly plump arthritic step down from the cart and on to the veranda. She greeted Eric, noticing the beer she remarked that Eric had started the pre-lunch drinks too early because by her reckoning lunch would be ready in one and half hours at about 1.30 pm. Eric responded jokingly that he was on holiday and relaxing and ready to take more beer before lunch. Lawyer Q-T got home at 1.15 pm and joined Eric on the veranda for his first bottle while Eric was on his second. They were both in a happy mood when lunch was announced. Lunch on a weekday at the Q-T household was usually a hurried affair for two, but for this afternoon it was for three as they were joined by Eric. Lawyer Q-T had carefully avoided the topic of Robyn while alone on the veranda with Eric because he preferred all talk about her to take place in the presence of Mrs Q-T. That way he was sure his wife would be in tune with him and privy to all his ideas regarding the delicate relationship with his niece. It is always easy going when the wife's relation is the long-staying house guest, but invariably awkward when the house is full of the husband's relatives. Ten minutes into lunch when Lawyer Q-T was sure the door to the kitchen was firmly shut he asked Eric whether he had spoken to Robyn since the events of yesterday's dinner and what were her reactions?

"We have spoken at length; she expressed genuine gratitude to both of you and was very happy about the new developments. I was happy to learn that she was not the ungrateful type."

"I already know what you have just told me. I want to know whether she was aware that you gingered us up to take that decision."

Eric protested, "I am not aware that I gingered you up, as far as I am concerned it is your own inherent good nature which encouraged you to take that decision and my plan is to thank the two of you in her presence and in the presence of the children to-night at dinner and you have spoilt that ceremony by taking the wind out of my sail."

"Eric this is not the time for hypocrisy, domestic diplomacy or deception: the truth is the truth, and to quote from John Keats, '*Truth is beauty and beauty is truth.*'"

To which Eric replied, "Uncle, I thought of you as a strictly pragmatic lawyer, I did not know you dabbled in the Arts and English Literature, I am impressed."

Mrs Q-T joined Eric to applaud the literary attributes of Uncle James who immediately spoke out, "I took my literary education very seriously, indeed I did a degree in English before I proceeded to do law and that interlude has not been in vain, it has always helped me to be ahead of my colleagues especially the sworn rivals most of whom are functional illiterates when it comes to the nuances of the English language, which after all is the medium by which we practise law in this country."

It was now the turn of Eric to speak. "I am not a hypocrite. Although I accept that I persuaded you a bit, the ease with which that persuasion took effect was what I wish to commend both of you for."

Mrs Q-T then said, "All is well that ends well."

Papa Lawyer waited for a second, expecting Eric to recognise the quotation. When he did not, he called his attention, and remarked how his literary attributes had obviously rubbed on to his dear wife. Eric was impressed but expressed his resentment about not having been encouraged or helped to follow the educational road map of his uncle. Lawyer Q-T quickly barged in and said that the family must not put all its eggs in the one basket of the Law profession as the 'B' family was doing. "

"Stonewall's philosophy was diversification and that was exactly what we are doing. That is why you are in business and already it is well known in financial circles that you are the wealthy one in the family and not my poor self."

They all laughed at the joke and Eric was flattered by the fact that his uncle James Quintin-Taki of all people had insinuated equality of uncle and nephew as regards success in their chosen professions. Lunch came to an end and they were all happy that they had taken the correct decision. Clever Robyn had eavesdropped and heard everything. Information which further convinced her that Eric was genuinely fond of her and she was very happy because the feeling was mutual.

Dinner that evening went on as planned. Eric thanked the whole family, namely Mr and Mrs Q-T, and their three children on behalf of Robyn, and advised Robyn to do the same. Robyn got up from her seat and went round to the head of the family, curtsied gracefully and thanked him. She turned round to face Mrs Q-T, called her by name curtsied smiled and thanked her. She then faced Eric looked at him eyeball-to-eyeball, curtsied and thanked him. Finally she faced her young cousins, mentioned their names in turn and thanked them. Mrs Q-T and the young ones lingered on at the table for small talk while the master of the house invited his nephew to the library for a glass of brandy over a cigar to wash down and facilitate the digestion of the sumptuous dinner, and small talk. The elderly lawyer expressed immense satisfaction at the progress his young nephew had made at Sekondi and wished him well. Eric in turn thanked his treasured uncle for the confidence and good will he had displayed towards him and promised not to relax but press on to achieve more success. Lawyer James then enquired about Eric's family. He told him that his wife was four months pregnant and she was currently in good hands because her mother was currently their house guest at Sekondi. Eric then stated that he would be leaving by the boat from Accra port the next day which information prompted to him say: "We must then retire to bed early and rest to face the busy morning that awaits us."

The two gentlemen then went to their bedrooms for what they both thought would be a good night's sleep, especially after the sips of excellent brandy with which they drove the dinner down, as it was the belief that a good brandy was the perfect antidote for heartburn especially when dinner was late.

Early to bed at 8.30 pm, yes, but sleep did not come easily to both gentlemen. On his part the older gentleman tossed and turned sleepless for several hours making his wife lying beside him anxious that he was worried about an impending catastrophe. When she finally plucked up courage and asked him what the matter was, he freely gave a detailed account of a misdemeanour he suspected he had committed. The sensible wife thought deeply and assured him that it was not that bad; together they formulated a strategy to take care of the of the problem, a strategy which included talking to the Chief Justice first thing in the morning. Lawyer James calmed down and was thus able to sleep soundly till morning.

Eric's problem which also triggered insomnia for several hours was of a different nature. Robyn his first cousin had no business awakening romantic feelings in him, but that was just what was happening. What really frightened him was that he suspected that it was mutual and that the young woman was also falling in love with him. Older women were usually sharp at noticing such things and already he had a hunch that although nothing had happened except the one episode of going to Robyn's room and innocently seeing her naked, Mrs Q-T had sensed a bond between him and his beautiful cousin. Eric did not like the manner in which throughout dinner last night the good lady constantly and alternately stared at him and then her as though she wanted to capture a secret flash of romantic communication between them. Eric was particularly careful and did not look in Robyn's direction even once during the whole period. Eric was also aware of the possibility that, for a wise old, experienced lady, it could be rather the avoidance of a glimpse between them which could have awakened her suspicion.

Indeed, she had in mind to call her husband's attention, but she shelved the idea because of his pre-occupation with professional problems which needed urgent solution. Besides whereas a professional reputation was at stake as regards the husband's problem, that of Eric and Robyn apart from being at the moment mere speculation, was at worst family gossip or scandal which must needs be nipped in the bud. She decided that it would be imprudent to dwell on a mere potential scandalous affair now when solid evidence was conspicuously lacking and there would be plenty of time yet to nip it. However, as things turned out she had made a mistake in underestimating the speed of events of the heart.

Eric on the other hand could not sleep for several hours as he struggled in vain to block out images and thoughts of Robyn from his mind. In one instance it felt like infatuation which he could deal with because same was usually short lived, on the other hand it could be love in which case he knew that there could be trouble in store because love tends to be stubborn and difficult to shake off. The girl no doubt was very beautiful and also possessed endearing and elegant mannerisms despite the paucity of her formal education. Late uncle Jeffery must have taken great pains to bring her only daughter up very well. Eric made a note to probe the secrets of the 'schooling' of Robyn by her late father. He recalled what she had already told him, that he hired a Sunday school teacher to give her extra lessons in reading and writing the Ga language well beyond ordinary Sunday school which dwelt mainly on reading of bible stories and learning of hymns. It was while speculating on the educational history of Robyn that he fell asleep. He slept deeply for a few hours, thanks to the several tots of after dinner brandy he had consumed in the library with his uncle. On waking up, he noticed that the house was very quiet and guessed that the house was empty. His pocket watch revealed that it was 8.15 am and, being a weekday, he knew that the master of the house had left at 7.30 am to work, and the madam too probably went out at 8.00 am to attend to family or trading business in the centre of town. The children had gone to school, the cook and her assistant had gone to market and the lazy gardener was probably still asleep in his hut or gone out on an errand. He suppressed any thoughts about Robyn because that could lead to dangerous adventures. He decided to continue snoozing for another hour because he was already packed for the journey and he would need only an hour to bathe, dress up, take a quick breakfast and get out of the house at 11.30 am in order to be at the Accra port for embarkation at 12 noon. He had already said goodbye to the whole household the day before at dinner. All he needed to do was carry his portmanteau to the main road outside the gate and hail a cab to convey him to the port which was only a 20- minute ride from the gate. He was just about snoozing again when he heard a soft knock on the door. He was not quite sure there was a real knock as he was still half asleep. He shook himself wide awake and listened attentively. The knock was repeated and this time he was sure it was a typical crafty feminine knock and he suspected that it could only be Robyn. He braced himself and answered.

"Come in, the door is not locked."

Robyn walked into the room wearing a long soft robe, not clinging to her body as such nevertheless all her generous curves were clearly visible. She looked exquisitely beautiful, literally breath-taking. She spoke first.

"This being your last day, I was waiting for you because I

thought you would like to see me, but since you did not come, I decided to come to find out what was keeping you away, maybe I have a secret rival who had crept in during the night."

Eric smiled and said, "A sense of humour in a beautiful girl is too much! Robyn indeed you are irresistible, lock the door and come closer."

She locked the door quietly and sauntered to the bedside. With a firm grip of her wrist and a deep breath, Eric pulled her on to the bed and then noticed that she had just come out of the bath wearing practically nothing under her long robe. The intimacy was spontaneous and very warm and fulfilment came mutually, absolutely and sweetly. As there was not much time to linger on, she said a hurried goodbye, jumped out of the bed and reminded him to write to her soon as previously arranged. She unlocked the door, crept out on to the quiet corridor and noiselessly rushed into the labyrinth of the big house.

BOAT TRIP TO SEKONDI

The boat sailed from Accra Port at exactly 12 noon and thus Eric was on his way to Sekondi. Having missed breakfast, he was hungry and made his way straight to the bar where he knew he could get a quick snack as lunch was not due to be served formally until 1.00 pm. He found a few people at the bar but he avoided all of them and looked for a lonely table in the far corner. He signalled the barman and ordered a club sandwich and a jug of beer. The beer tasted good, and the sandwich was tasty and filling. Soon the bar filled up with several travellers all excited by the impending voyage along the Gold Coast. Some like him only to Sekondi but others were bound to faraway places such as Monrovia, Freetown, Las Palmas, or even to Liverpool. The first stop would be at Winneba 30 miles as the crow flies west from Accra.

Lunch on the boat was served at 1.00 pm. It was a sort of brunch of mixed African and European cuisine and lasted for 45 minutes. There were unlimited quantities of food beer and wines. The sea was very calm and the passenger liner although big enough to sail the high seas kept close to the coastline which was clearly visible from port side throughout this part of the voyage. After lunch passengers on the upper decks strolled on the deck or rested on chairs in the lounges or on the deck. All those on several day-voyages and the few on short day trips like Eric had been allocated cabins to which they returned for siesta. He retired into a small cabin which he shared with another second-class passenger for siesta. As the ship cruised at approximately 10 miles an hour, they arrived at Winneba Port at 3.00 pm. Passengers were allowed to go on shore if they so desired for 30 minutes. Departure from Winneba was at 4.00 pm for the next stage of the journey which was to Cape Coast approximately 60 miles away. Knowing what lay in store at Cape Coast where the night reveries were famous, Eric continued his siesta. He slept intermittently, rocked gently by the smooth sailing boat while he kept an eye every now and then on his pocket watch. At 6.30 pm he woke up, washed up, changed into a decent light weight cream evening jacket and a matching shirt and wandered into the dining room at 7.30 pm. A long programme lay ahead. The elaborate dinner of several courses each accompanied by the appropriate wine started at 8.00 pm. At 9.00 pm there was live music for dancing while the dining continued. The boat arrived and anchored at Cape Coast for those who had come to the end of their journey to disembark on to small but sturdy and comfortable boats to the port on firm land. The same small boats returned to the ship shortly after, full of fun loving middle upper classes people from Cape Coast to join the dinner and dance party which was scheduled to end long after mid-night. The dance and dinner party were elevated to a fever pitch of great fun and enjoyment by the Cape Coast clientele but as the popular saying goes 'every good thing has an end.' The dance dinner party ended at 1.30 am and the boats were ready to take the fun people back to Cape Coast. The ship set sail for the last part of journey to Sekondi at 2.00 am. The distance ahead was approximately 40 miles and the scheduled time of arrival was 6.00 am, that left approximately 3 hours for sleeping which was exactly what Eric did. Back in the cabin he jumped into bed and slept soundly up to 30 minutes before arrival. There was just enough time for a quick breakfast of tea and buttered toast before disembarkation. Waiting for Eric at the arrival hall was a sizeable welcoming party consisting of his good wife, her parents, employees from the port, the shipping agency and retail shops and to his pleasant surprise a few friends, white and black, from the Sekondi club. There was great joy in all their faces and he was deeply touched by the solidarity and goodwill on display. He was flattered that so many people were so happy to see him having been away for only four weeks. They all trooped to the house where an elaborate brunch had been prepared. His plan to go to work had to be abandoned, thus disrupting his attempt to catch up with the backlog of four weeks. The prevailing atmosphere rendered his plans quite inappropriate and in the end he decided to go along with the majority. The welcoming party ended at 3.00 pm. His body was tired enough to demand a siesta. At exactly 5.00 pm he woke up and had a quick shower, put on smart casual clothes, and was on his way to the club at 6.00 pm where another party awaited him. The evening at the club was exceptionally pleasant. A good buffet dinner had been laid on with wines, followed by after dinner brandy, Cuban cigars and strong Turkish coffee for which the club was well known. The soiree at the club was of course a family affair so most members including were accompanied by their wives. The soiree ended relatively early at 1.00 am because the following day was a full working day.

The day was ushered in by the bright morning sun rays through the bedroom window at 5.45 am. It was in early March and the weather was changing to the hot season after the cool dry harmattan. Eric was in a hurry to see the office and shops after being away on holiday for one month in Accra. On his way to the office he saw the same familiar faces and the same scenes which reassured him that he had not been away for too long. He got the same feeling at the port. The clerks were already at work and looking very business-like as usual. The chief clerk followed him to his office and after a brief welcome started briefing him. Eric suddenly realised how very efficient Mr Quampah was and made a mental note to give him a generous bonus at Christmas and to promote him to Manager in the new year.

Curiosity got the better part of him in that as soon as Quampah left the office he wanted to know more about this efficient elderly man he had inherited from the original European owner of the shipping company which his uncle had helped him to purchase. He pulled Quampah's file from the cabinet and read carefully from the first entry. Mr Quampah had joined the firm straight from leaving secondary school in Cape Coast as an assistant clerical officer and risen slowly through the ranks to his present position as chief clerk, the highest position he could rise to by decree of British Colonial policy. A rank above chief clerk took one to the managerial level and would have been possible for Mr Quampah had he been white or European. Eric realised that as a black African his position in the firm as the owner or managing director or even just the boss of Mr Quampah was anomalous. All his previous bosses had been young semi-literate inexperienced white 'boys'.

Lawyer Q-T had confided in him on several occasions in the past that the Colonial Secretary acting through the Governor of the Gold Coast resented the idea that a mere black man was the ostensible manager of a company, a position which by right and British Colonial policy belonged to a white European whether educated or not, trained or not, well-mannered or not. He stated that as a lawyer he knew how to play the waiting game being aware of the fact that no situation, especially if man made, was permanent. But so far, so good, the company was doing good business and prospering.

Although Eric had a lot of white friends at the Esikado Coast club, he knew that they all belonged to working classes of Britain, Europe and South Asia. They were white but riff raff holding blue colour non-executive posts such as tally clerks, foremen at construction sites, sanitary inspectors, cashiers etc. The real white elite of Sekondi moved in the circles of the District Commissioner (DC) who represented the colonial Governor in the capital Accra. The white elite belonged to the Sekondi Club whose legitimate membership was exclusively white. They were the heads of departments of government establishments, managing directors of large trading companies such as U.A.C., U.T.C., P.Z., S.A.T., G. B. Ollivant, A. G. Leventis, managers of large shipping companies such as Elder Dempster Lines, managers of companies engaged in the export of timber, gold, diamond, manganese and bauxite all extracted from the hinterland. The few black members of the Coast or Esikadu club who had had a glimpse at the white Sekondi Club albeit by default knew that the Coast club was a poor mediocre version of the real thing. Eric himself being relatively new to Sekondi society had never been to the Sekondi club simply because he had never been invited. He suddenly realised that as a businessman there were things he did know because they were done on his blind side because he had no close allies in the elite business community. After some hard thinking he came to the conclusion that Quampah was just the ally or spy he needed. The man possessed excellent qualities; he was intelligent and unobtrusive yet keenly observant and unpretentious with above all a good sense of humour making him universally popular. Eric decided on a three-step plan. The first step would entail inviting him to his office for a long talk in order to get acquainted with the detailed social history of corporate and colonial Sekondi. The second stage would be to sponsor him to join the Coast club from which he had hitherto been excluded because he could not afford it. The last stage would be to set him up as a spy.

Eric used the weekend to perfect his plans. On arrival at his office Monday morning the first thing he did was to summon Quampah to his office for a discussion. Prior to actually calling him, he pulled his file from the cabinet and studied it very closely, indeed memorised it and put it back. All he had on his desk as Quampah walked in were his pen, ink and a clean sheet of paper for taking notes, thus making sure that there was no variation from what took place at previous meetings. The discussion was successful in that it served the purpose for which it was intended. Quampah responded to all the issues raised with candour and in a relaxed manner. On the matter of how vital corporate and civil information seeped through the grape vine even to the DC and the Governor of the colony, he was aware that there were professional and casual informers black and white operating at all levels. He volunteered the information that indeed the seemingly liberal mixed Coast club Eric belonged to was the most important hub for gathering information. He was aware (while Eric was not) that there were ostensibly white members who belonged secretly to both the mixed Coast and pure white Sekondi club. Eric saw his chance to launch his strategy and proceeded cautiously as follows.

"Mr Quampah, for the sake of our business which is constantly under threat because the management is not white, I must know what is happening and the only way to do that would be to identify the poor whites who belong to both clubs. I would like to sponsor you to join the Coast club and try to use your good offices and corporate skills not only to identify those dual members but also what they are up to. It is a very delicate assignment needing discretion and patience because no clues must be left for suspicion."

Mr Quampah's reaction proved beyond all reasonable doubt that he understood the assignment. He said, "It is a good task and a challenge which can be surmounted."

"Have you any question on any of the issues we have discussed or on any other issues?"

"Yes sir," he answered in a rather jovial mood and continued, "I thought I had been summoned to a promotion interview but I am not quite sure of that anymore."

The guy really had a good sense of humour and Eric burst out laughing and said that it was indeed a promotion exercise but only the part one which he had obviously passed, for the final part his uncle the lawyer and part owner of the business would be present because from his present position of chief clerk, the next stage would be managerial and therefore a European post. This line of conversation opened a new chapter because Quampah divulged that it would be the second interview with lawyer Q-T on the panel because when he got the job several years ago the panel consisted of the original owner and managing director Mr Mitter himself, lawyer Q-T who was then the corporate lawyer of the firm and family friend of Mr Mitter and last but not the least the company secretary, a white man called Mr Demper who took notes. Eric asked Mr

Quampah to narrate what happened on that occasion because although his uncle had referred to those times on several occasions he had never gone into details. When Eric looked and saw that time was far spent, he postponed the narrative and closed the meeting.

CHAPTER TWO

Mrs Elsa Wuta delivered a bouncing baby boy (the couple's second son) on Wednesday morning in July and the out-dooring ceremony was performed according to Ga custom exactly one week after the baby was born. The baby was named after Eric's father Nii Yartei Wuta. The ceremony was performed by elderly members of the Wuta family some of whom had travelled all the way from Kpone, a coastal fishing village about 25 miles East of Accra and had arrived by boat on the previous day. It was a joyous occasion with plenty to eat and drink despite the fact that it was a working day.

The Ga-Dangbe people of South-Eastern Ghana had always been stubborn when it came to strict adherence to their traditional customs and no amount of opposition whether from Europeans or other fellow Africans could push then to abandon their well-developed, deeply entrenched ceremonies. Ironically the same groups who through lack of understanding opposed the ceremonies were notorious for enjoying them and always waited anxiously for the next invitation be it to Homowo or Kpodziemo (baby outdooring), Gblashibimo (engagement for marriage), Naadzormo (celebration of the good life during the lifetime of the celebrant) and many more.

The mother of the new born baby being from Cape Coast, her relatives came to the ceremony in large numbers and were overwhelmed and intrigued by the complexity and joy of the ceremony to such an extent that while the older ones were stunned with jealousy wondering where the Gas got this from and why their ancestors had not handed over anything like this to them, the young unmarried women were so impressed that they promised their parents that they would surely marry the next eligible Ga man who came their way. The ceremony

“Kpodziemɔ” Outdooring and naming of baby boy one week after birth

started early when the sun had just come up. The baby who prior to that occasion had been kept indoors was brought outdoors for the first time, shown day light, introduced to the Almighty God whose blessings for long life and prosperity were implored for the new-born through a long poetic prayer which ended with admonitions to the baby to be of good behaviour and to work hard so that those around might enjoy some of the fruits of his labour. The baby boy was then named as tradition demanded after the line of his paternal grandparents. Since his paternal grandfather was also a second son of his father the new-born baby boy was named after him as follows:

The presiding elder shouted loudly for attention, "Agooo!!!"

There was a spontaneous equally loud response from the congregation,

"Ameee!!!!"

There was complete silence, and one could literally hear a pin drop. The presiding elder then spoke,

"Let me warn all of you here gathered on this our ancestral Wednesday that the new-born baby, this new visitor is not nameless to be addressed to as 'kwe' or 'hei you there.' He has a name. His name is Nii Yartei. My assistant will come around and serve each of you a tot of the naming drink which you will sip after he is sure that you have mastered the name and can pronounce it correctly. The naming process was followed by showers of gifts in cash and assorted items from all assembled. Each donor was clearly identified by full name, title, credentials, relationship to the new-born, either parents, or friend of family, colleague at work, or neighbour. The showering of gifts was interspersed with traditional entertainment and music, jokes, drinks, cookies, cakes and so on and went on all morning well into the afternoon so that both breakfast and lunch were served. Guests who had to go to work stayed only for short periods, while the others who were not so committed stayed put and enjoyed themselves all day.

Eric's mother of course had seized the opportunity to come to Sekondi and she was glad she came because that was the first time she had seen her son's new abode. She was naturally overjoyed, and she relished every moment of her new status of a proud grandmother. Elsie's mother was also there.

As Elsa the baby's maternal grandmother was available to help with the baby, Eric's mother had lots of opportunities for long uninterrupted interactions with her son. She gave detailed accounts of all that was happening at the homestead in Accra. Lawyer Q-T's household was naturally the most important topic as far as Mrs. Catherine Wuta (nee Quinton-Taki) was concerned. The elderly lady adored her younger brother and admired all his achievements including the latest which she reported to Eric at length and in great detail. The most important news item was the fact that her brother had been nominated by the Governor to represent Accra Central in the Legislative Council of the Gold Coast Colony. His name had been sent to the King at Buckingham Palace after vetting at Whitehall where he had received unanimous approval by acclamation: such was the fame of Eric's uncle in faraway London. The ceremony itself was to take place at the Christiansborg Castle at the end of the legal vacation, specifically on the last Friday in September 1900. The future Legislative Council member had already been informed by official letter from London and he had accepted in writing. The honour of course came along with some expenses such that only the very well to do citizens of the Gold Coast Colony could afford to accept and Uncle James Quinton-Taki was certainly the best example of such worthy natives of this British Colony.

Eric's mother then proudly announced that preparations had already begun and the prescribed attire for each of the several members of the future Legislator's family had already been ordered from Europe. At that stage of the conversation Eric's mother stated emphatically that she had been given the mandate to formally invite Eric to the ceremony. She also showed Eric the pro forma invoice of the formal wear which Lawyer Q-T had ordered from London. It was a tall list which included tailcoats, white ties, dress shirts and formal black shoes for the Lawyer-Legislator himself and his only close male adult relative Eric Nortey Wuta. Eric exclaimed "Hurray" and recollected the last time they met, his uncle had wanted to know the size of his suit, shirt and even shoes and he thought his uncle was trying to assess whether he could pass on some of his suits to him for church on Sundays, because the last time Q-T wanted Eric to accompany him to church he realised that Eric had no suit worthy of the occasion. Formal day and evening frocks had also been ordered for the family ladies. The list was handed to Eric and he quickly read aloud,

"Mrs Quinton-Taki, Mrs Catherine Wuta (nee Quinton-Taki), Miss Robyn Quinton-Taki," Eric paused and asked, "Robyn is on the list?"

Eric's mother then answered with exasperation, "But of course! Your cousin Robyn is now a recognised precious member of our family. The good work you started casually has yielded wonderful fruits. Robyn is learning fast at the night school and she now not only speaks but writes good English and Ga. In addition, she attends Mrs Lamptey's famous vocational school of fashion. She is already a first-class designer and also a good seamstress. She has mastered the modern tailoring machine and she is earning a handsome salary. Her designs and finished products are very popular. When she learned that I was coming to Sekondi for the out-dooring of your son, she designed and tailored six baby boy outfits and parcelled them to be delivered to your wife. She also designed and tailored two lady's shirts for your wife, and I hereby present them to you from your talented cousin Robyn."

Eric was touched and felt very guilty for not having bothered to reply the three letters he had received from Robyn in the past three months. The first two letters were written in Ga, the last one in elementary English. Finally, Mrs Wuta itemised the time frame of the forthcoming events as follows: The actual ceremony would come on in the last week of September 1900, the last Saturday of the legal vacation so that business in the high courts could start in earnest on the following Monday. The ceremonies will last 2 weeks climaxing on the last day Saturday of September. The plan was that Eric would travel to Accra on the steam mail boat scheduled to depart from Liverpool carrying the official Colonial Office dignitaries who would be helping the Governor to perform the ceremony in Accra. Eric was therefore advised to prepare to embark on that boat when it docked at Sekondi. Indeed, the booking had already been done and the ticket was handed over there and then to Eric by his mother.

Eric knew that the circumstances were such that his wife must be fully informed without delay. Therefore, that very evening he outlined the impending programme to his wife, and he was grateful to God that he had an understanding wife who did not hesitate to come to the conclusion that Eric would have to travel without her. Although she loved going out to high society functions, she knew that the timing was wrong in that her duty was to remain at home and take care of their brand-new baby boy.

CHAPTER THREE

ACCRA CELEBRATIONS

The long-expected trip to Accra was near, and Eric was quite nervous about it. He had been very reluctant to talk about it with his wife Elsa because for once he felt guilty that he was going to leave her at home alone with their little precious one. On this particular day in late August, he plucked up courage to discuss the situation with his wife. "By the way Elsa, do you realise that less than a fortnight from now I will be going to Accra for my uncle's elevation to the Legislative Council?"

"Of course, I am aware, and I have observed all the preparations you have so far made."

Eric was taken aback, but he recovered quickly and said jovially:

"My dear wife if you are really so up to date then tell me the preparations I have made."

"My dear husband I am aware that you have already been in touch with my mother in Cape Coast to come to Sekondi next week to help me look after baby.

Oh that! But I did that with your blessing several weeks ago indeed soon after we heard the news and even before my mother went back to Accra after the out-dooring of Kuku. What other preparations have you observed apart from that?"

Elsie answered his question.

"I am well aware and indeed reluctantly eavesdropped on the secret meeting you had in this very house with Mr Quampah. I know all the decisions you took! Must I recite them?"

"No," said Eric, "enough is enough! say no more, you have proved your point. But then if you know so much, why have you been so quiet about the old man's affairs? Don't you want to rejoice with the family of your husband over such a distinguished achievement?"

"Of course, I do rejoice, you of all people know very well that Uncle James is my favourite as a result of the part he played in the generation of our marriage. He persuaded your mother to accept me despite being a typical 'flighty Fante woman' as your mother used to describe her future daughter in law."

"But I thought you get on well with my mother."

"Now I do, but the beginning was very difficult."

"Let bygones be bygones, let us face current events. I will be away for about a month and your mother has kindly agreed to come to Sekondi for the whole period. Is that not very nice of her?"

"My mother is a very nice woman and I can assure you we will be well looked after."

To which Eric replied, "I thank the Almighty God for providing me with good loving and understanding wife and superb and kind mother-in-law."

SEA TRIP FROM SEKONDI TO ACCRA

Sunday evening, a day in September 1900 saw the arrival at Sekondi Port of the luxurious Mail boat which had sailed from Liverpool 12 days earlier with the representative of the British Colonial Secretary and the Governor of the Gold Coast on board as VIP passengers. The Governor had gone on a short vacation to London to enable him, as protocol demanded, to accompany high British government officials led by the Colonial Secretary to the Gold Coast to perform an important governance ceremony. As usual on such occasions crowds of local residents stood by to watch the spectacle of the disembarkation of the important white colonial masters and their dispatch in convoy to the District Commissioner's Residency at Sekondi Ridge. The port was busy all night and the greater part of the following day discharging imported heavy machinery and equipment for the gold, diamond and manganese mining companies of the interior. The off-loading ended late afternoon followed immediately by embarkation of goods and passengers scheduled to travel eastwards to ports of the Gold Coast such as Cape Coast and Accra and beyond to Lagos, Port Harcourt and as far as Cameroon where the boat would turn around for its return journey. The Royal party from the UK embarked formally at 6.00 pm on Tuesday and the ship sailed from Sekondi port shortly afterwards. Eric was part of the VIP embarkation party which joined the Royal party which had resided and spent Monday night at the Residency. The sea trip to Accra was fast as there were no stops on the way, and uneventful.

The boat arrived in the waters of Accra port in the early hours of Thursday morning but disembarkation was deliberately delayed for protocol to apply. The ceremony of disembarkation started at 9.00 am and practically involved all those who mattered in British Accra. The time of year had been carefully selected; the third week of September to be exact when there were usually no rains, quite sunny but still cool because of the lingering of the cold cloudy light showers of August. The ceremony was very colourful. Apart from the presence of the colonial secretary and his white colleagues all formally dressed, local chiefs colourfully robed in rich kente robes and golden ornaments and headgear graced the occasion. The climax of the welcome was when the Governor of the Gold Coast Colony helped the Royal representative ashore from the Governor's boat which had conveyed them from the ocean liner which had anchored in deep waters far from the beach. The two travellers were welcomed onto the red carpet by the colonial secretary who had

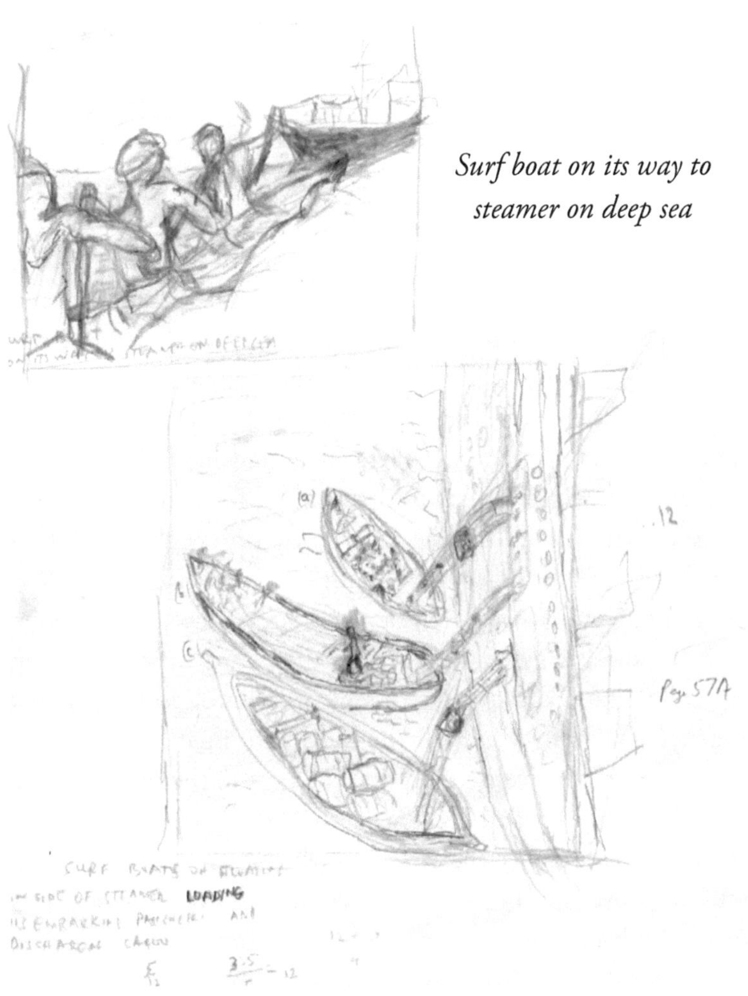

Surf boat on its way to steamer on deep sea

Surf boat at side of steamer, loading disembarking passengers and discharging cargo

acted as chief administrator while the Governor was away. The delegation from London was introduced to the local dignitaries lined up according to rank, the British national anthem was struck, the Union Jack was unfurled, raised and saluted before the delegates entered the carriages for the drive-in convoy to the Christiansborg Castle, the residence of the Governor for another welcoming ceremony and official luncheon. That evening it was the turn of the Colonial Secretary to play host to the visiting dignitaries, members of the Legislative Council and their spouses, prominent Paramount Chiefs, senior civil servants, the Chief Medical Officer, Inspector General of Police and heads of important British and European Commercial and Mining Firms. To this reception were also invited the newly nominated or appointed members of the Gold Coast Legislative Council and their spouses. It was a good opportunity for the new members to meet those who mattered in the governance of the Colony. The guests trooped in, all formally dressed for the social occasion. They were first treated to cocktails, during which introductions to the dignitaries were made and old acquaintances renewed. Dinner was announced with a gong at 7.30 pm. The guests were shown their seats which had been carefully arranged according to rank and station in the colonial order. It was only when all the local elite including the new council members were seated that the host in the person of the Colonial Secretary and his wife led the dignitaries including the Royal representative, the British Parliamentary representative and the Governor on to the elevated head table. The occupants of the high table were all white. On the few occasions in the past when black African upstarts had complained about this arrangement, retribution was swift by banishing them into oblivion. The British National anthem was played by the well-schooled police band discretely tucked away from view and all stood up; guests who were in uniform added colour by saluting in the usual manner. An elaborate four course dinner with the

Citizens of Accra waiting to welcome visiting dignitaries from England

choicest French wines was served. Speeches were deliberately short and kept to the minimum. The host welcomed his guest with a few brief sentences and sat down. That was the signal for the Governor to formally welcome the visiting dignitaries by name and rank, stating the purpose of their visit by alluding to the tasks scheduled for the following day. He ended by proposing a toast first to His Majesty the King: all and sundry stood up and drank deeply to the King's health; he then proposed the second toast to the Royal representative in their midst and his distinguished entourage. The Duke of Kent then stood up and thanked the Governor and his loyal subjects. Within seconds the side drummer rattled the introduction and the police band repeated *God Save the King* to signal the end of the dinner.

THE LEGISLATIVE COUNCIL CEREMONY

Friday morning arrived at last, and the Q-T household was turned into a beehive. The occupants had gone to bed late because of the endless stream of visitors, family members and well-wishers who needed to be received and entertained on the eve of Lawyer James Quinton-Taki's elevation. Whereas the previous day's dinner was necessarily restricted to high officials and the new Council members only, the one a few hours away would be open to the general public with the proviso that invited guest would be seated inside the hall while the bulk of the people would be outside the hall, eager to catch a glimpse at the important guests on their entry and exit. On the previous day Mr and Mrs Quinton-Taki had attended the Colonial Secretary's welcoming dinner party alone. Not even Mr Eric Wuta, business tycoon of Sekondi was allowed to accompany them. However, all those they left behind dutifully dressed up for the household soiree and received the several family members and friends whether invited or not. The crowd waited

Chief of James Town welcome the Duke of Kent

patiently for their hero and his wife and when they arrived home they were received with loud hurrahs and prolonged spontaneous hand clapping. The arrival of the famous couple was the cue to the start of the house party which turned out to be as elaborate and sumptuous as that hosted by the Colonial Secretary. The joy of the occasion was such that it rendered all and sundry rather euphoric. This included Papa James himself who had an important appointment next morning. Thus, they retired to bed after 3.00 am which meant they had less than 2 hours of rest before they were woken up at 5.00 am to prepare for the important occasion.

Despite the two hours of rest, the flow of adrenaline was so high that preparations proceeded at optimum pace and they were all ready to quit the house on time. The two gentlemen of the household, namely the newly proposed Legislative Councillor James Quinton-Taki and his young nephew and budding business tycoon Eric Wuta looked smart and sartorially correct in their made-to-measure London tail suits and white dress shirts and white bow ties to match. For this occasion, the ladies of the household namely the wife of the new Legislative Councillor Mrs Quinton-Taki, the sister Mrs Wuta senior, the niece Miss Robyn Quinton-Taki, and the teenage daughter Miss Kate Quinton-Taki wore different shades of dark two-piece business suits ordered from London for the occasion. The twin sons of Councillor Quinton-Taki were equally well attired in their London tailored dark striped trousers, navy breast coats and matching ties on white shirts over which they wore smartly tailored dark blazers. There was a professional photographer at hand to take several photos especially the group family one for the records before the ride to the Legislative Council hall. They arrived there in good time and they were directed to their reserved seats by 9.35 am. The Councillor was directed to the VIP room to join the other dignitaries. They observed that no

James and Elsa Quinton-Taki and family all dressed up for the function at the Legislative Assembly

sooner had they been seated than the gallery seats rapidly filled up with equally well-dressed invited guests and relatives of old, current and new Councillors. At about 9.50 am the Councillors started trooping to their seats in the Council chamber below. They were all seated by 9.58 am. At 10.00 am on the dot there was a loud announcement instructing all assembled to stand up to receive the dignitaries. The dignitaries were followed into the chamber by the newly nominated members, and all remained standing for the British national anthem which was powerfully rendered by the Gold Coast Police Band. All sat and bowed down their heads for a solemn opening prayer by the Bishop of Accra. All sat and the formal opening of the Gold Coast Legislative Council was conducted by the Governor of the Colony himself. He formally welcomed the representative of the King in the person of the Duke of Kent, the direct cousin of the reigning monarch and a royal in his own right. The governor then welcomed the rest of the delegation from London including the cabinet Minister in charge of British Colonial affairs, and finally a long list of local officials, paramount Chiefs, clan elders and all invited guests. The clerk of the house outlined the short agenda. The first item at the beginning of a new session was of course the King's speech which was very brief and ably delivered by his representative for the occasion the Duke of Kent. He communicated to the Council members and all his loyal subjects of the Gold Coast his warm greetings and wished them success in all their undertakings especially the main business of the day which was to swear in the new members whom he identified individually by name and congratulated. The brilliantly delivered Royal speech was enthusiastically received and earned a spontaneous standing ovation from all and sundry. The next item was the official admission and swearing-in of the new Legislative Council members. The dignified ceremony was performed by the Royal representative himself ably supported by the

Governor of the Colony, the Cabinet Minister and the Chief Justice who administered the oath. The Governor addressed the new councillors, the head of the Gold Coast Civil service also known as Colonial Secretary gave the vote of thanks and the meeting was adjourned for lunch for invited guests only at the Governor's residence at Christiansborg Castle.

SATURDAY AFFAIRS

It is an axiom universally acknowledged that every large township or community all over the world develops or creates a character or culture peculiar to its people, especially in their work and play habits. Accra, at the turn of the nineteenth to twentieth century, was no exception. In Accra of those days, the culture was strictly '*all work and no play* makes Tei a dull boy' which implied that each of the seven days of the week was strictly assigned to work or play. It was the unwritten rule that all must work hard and play hard. Fishermen thus set off to sea at early dawn every day of the week except Tuesday, which was by custom religiously celebrated as their day of rest and recreation; except that around mid-morning after a heavy breakfast of hot banku and spicy peppery fresh fish light soup (better known to fisher folk as *nsashua*), instead of going to sleep (as the older ones invariably did) the younger fishermen sauntered off to the airy beaches, spread their nets to dry in the sun, inspected them for defects (gaping holes) which they skilfully mended amid a joyous atmosphere of melodious drum music and dancing. The dancing was colourfully embellished by the local beautiful young women, experts in wriggling and gyrating well-developed anatomical endowments which never failed to please and attract the young men all the way to marriage.

Fishing boats and nets being mended

Those of the same stock who settled further inland, remote from the seashore, became farmers and worked equally hard at tilling the fertile land. They worked from dawn to dusk every day of the week except Friday, which was their day of absolute rest. When white men and women arrived in Accra, they engaged in several activities including the introduction of a brand-new religion Christianity which they preached intensively, resulting in the conversion of most but not all the people. The new religion insisted that all its converts reserved Sunday for Christian worship in church, followed by rest or abstention from work. Saturday became special for its role in anticipation of Sunday which must be devoted to meditation, worship and avoidance of all unholy activities.

The Saturday celebrations usually started after mid-day. Saturday afternoons became reserved for competitive sports followed by jubilations from early evening, continuing all night to the early hours of Sunday morning. Therefore, it did not surprise those who were well-versed about the culture of the citizens of Accra that, after an important Legislative Assembly business lasting a whole week, Saturday would be devoted to hard play in the afternoon and serious partying in the evening and throughout the night. On that Saturday afternoon, the children, young men and women from poor homes did their usual. They went to the beech to swim, surf and play on the sands. The idle rich, on the other hand, did what they enjoyed best: spending money at the racecourse on the outskirts of town. The Accra Turf Club owned the Racecourse where they gathered to enjoy horse racing and serious gambling. For the ongoing festive occasion, the Turf Club had planned a special season of four Saturdays of races, culminating on the Saturday immediately following the Friday Legislative Assembly events. The final race was to be an eight-furlong race to celebrate the occasion with the Governor's Cup at stake.

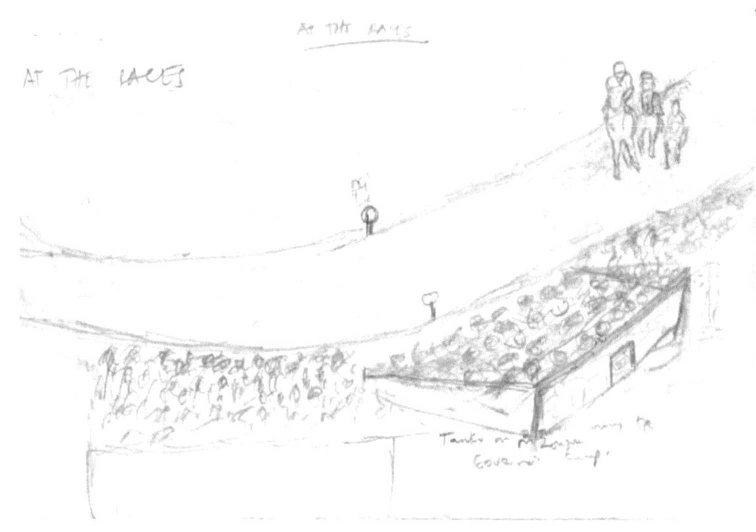

At the racecourse. Tanko on Victory Day winning the Governor's Cup

The Saturday mornings and mid-mornings of Governor's Cup day were always special in Accra. The stables where the racehorses were kept were situated on the outskirts of the city namely western at Korle Gonno, eastern at rural Osu, north-western at Abossey Okine/Kaneshie and north-eastern at rural Adabraka and Nima. (The first rather small racecourse was built in James Town near the Korle Lagoon, soon after a bigger and more popular one was built at between Tudu and Victoriaborg, where the horses were to be raced on the festive occasion at hand.) The lucky jockeys and trainers, knowing that the stakes were high, had put the selected horses through rigorous training all week up to Friday afternoon.

Activities resumed with gusto very early Saturday morning in all the appointed stables after the obligatory good night rest. The horses earmarked for the day's races were fed, thoroughly brushed, groomed and saddled with polished brown leathers and shiny metallic paraphernalia. Each horse had its name and colours. Well-dressed in their appropriate colours, they trooped ever so slowly and majestically from their abodes, ridden by apprentice jockeys under the watchful eyes of the trainers on foot close by in a leisurely and deliberate manner, to attract the attention of the numerous spectators lining up the routes the routes all over Accra towards the racecourse from as early as 9 am. By 11 am they were all safely latched on their paddocks in the racecourse under the watchful eyes of the stewards to make sure that none were drugged to enhance their performance beyond their range of capabilities which had been previously assessed, classified and duly recorded by experts.

The racing enthusiasts popularly known as pundits started trooping into the racecourse at 11.30 am, while the idle rich and dignitaries arrived smartly dressed (gentlemen) and fashionably attired (ladies) at 12 noon and immediately gravitated to the

Winning jockey receiving the Governor's Cup from Colonial Secretary

lounges and bars for relaxation and drinks and gossip to get into the mood for the occasion. Five races were usually scheduled for an afternoon, each contested by 10 to 20 horses belonging to class 5, 4, 3, 2 and 1 respectively at 2.30, 3.00, 3.30 ,4.00 and 5.00 pm promptly. On this particular festive occasion, the Governor's Cup was at stake for the last race at 5.00 pm. It was to be run on a flat hurdle free course for a distance of one mile or 8 furlongs, as the local pundits preferred to call it. At 4.30 pm the division-one horses and their jockeys were lined up for inspection in the paddocks. They were then inspected by experts including veterinary surgeons, to make sure that the horses were fit to race the distance and that they had not been doped. The jockeys did not escape scrutiny; their weights were checked to ensure that each jockey plus the added weight in his side pocket added up to the prescribed handicap prescribed for his horse.

Soon after the paddock inspection, the jockeys in their colourful livery mounted their horses and trooped majestically to the starting point where they were immediately put under the starter's orders behind a restraining net. The starter, with precision, pulled a string which mechanically raised the net far above the heads of the mounted jockeys' heads and the race was on. The game of Kings was always exciting. Pundits crowded on the fences overlooking the racetrack, shouting and cheering their favourite horses. The final bend – always dangerous – was soon negotiated safely and they all raced towards the winning post at great thundering speed, bundled together as though there was not going to be a clear winner. Lo and behold the race was over, and there was a clear winner to the naked eye of all observers rendering resort to photo-finish snap totally irrelevant.

The short ceremony of the presentation of the magnificent Governor's Cup was performed soon after the official declaration of the winning horse. On this occasion, the visiting British Colonial Secretary presented the magnificent Governor's Cup to the winning team of horse owner (Mr Ataa Nmai), jockey Nii Boifio, horse trainer Numo Ablade and last but not least the winning horse popularly nicknamed 'Victory Day' amidst deafening applause and obvious jubilation by the lucky who had won handsomely, because the winning horse was not the favourite. As custom demanded, the presentation was immediately followed by cocktails and a sumptuous dinner for the distinguished visitors local invited dignitaries and members of the Accra Turf Club whose president was the host. Farewell after dinner speeches brought the formal events to a successful happy ending and a sigh of relief to the organisers.

The departure on Tuesday morning for Sekondi was optional so that those who had business or family duties in Accra could pursue same. Eric was obliged to stay on because he had been assigned an important duty by his uncle Q-T and the family elders. He was to be the leader of a delegation made up of himself, his mother, an aunt from the family house in the centre of town and last but not the least Robyn as guide. Their duty was to go and inspect and assess the extent of the estate of the late Jeffrey Q-T the father of Robyn. Although in his will he had left everything to Robyn, the deed would be effective in 4 years when Robyn attained the majority age of 21; in the interim the Family with Q-T as head was deemed to be in charge.

They left Accra by horse and carriage early Tuesday morning hoping to arrive at Pakro near Mangoase deep in the hinterland of the Eastern province of the Gold Coast by dusk on the same day, barring any mishaps on the way. It was quite a long

Departure from Q-T Mansions for Pakro Farms

journey, even more so because they were obliged to stop briefly for rest and refreshment at Nsawam and then at Suhum where they procured fresh horses in exchange of the tired ones. They arrived at Pakro on schedule at 6.00 pm and as a telegram had been dispatched the previous day to the caretaker of the estate, they were expected, and a place had been prepared for them. They had their evening meal after a warm bath and sat amongst the local people in the cool moon-lit compound for friendly small talk spiced with witty village humour. There was plenty of sweet fresh palm wine for those who wanted some, but all the city visitors including Eric declined because of previous unpleasant experiences of diarrhoea and terrible hangovers.

The city folk had brought their own cartons of bottled beer for the gentlemen and lemonade for the ladies, having been warned that on no account should they touch the local drinks of palm wine and akpeteshie distilled all over rural Gold Coast from the finest sugar cane. Before they left Accra, Q-T emphasised that he had nothing against the local alcoholic beverages which the colonial British authorities had declared illegal, neither was it his policy to cripple indigenous business, however since they were being sent on a special and important assignment, it was their duty to remain healthy and of sound mind in order to accomplish their task satisfactorily. He toned down his stern warning by adding that perhaps when the work was completed and a full report written, they could indulge themselves and join the usual village merry making. They should also remember that the villagers were hardy and totally immune to the local germs and pollutants. Having been so well brainwashed by Q-T, the visitors from the city refused to be coerced to imbibe the palm wine and akpeteshie which were available in large quantities. The elderly and wise among the villagers concluded that the townsfolk took their assigned work seriously and respected them for it; on the contrary, the young and frivolous among the villagers mocked the townsfolk referring to them as chickens and children for their inability to enjoy adult pastimes such as drinking good palm wine and strong akpeteshie.

Earlier on, soon after their arrival at the farmhouse and before the evening frolicks described above, the intelligent and indefatigable overseer had shown them around the estate and allocated them rooms. Robyn was grief stricken especially when they were shown the locked room of her father. It was the entrenched tradition of the Ga people of the Gold Coast that the private chamber of the deceased must be securely locked with all its contents intact and undisturbed for a year. The ceremony of entering the chamber one year after the death of the father of Robyn the late Jeffrey Quinton-Taki was the purpose of the delegation's trip all the way from Accra to Pakro. Robyn was of course assigned to her old room which was next door to her late father's suite which as custom demanded had been securely locked since his death a little over a year ago. Robyn's aunts namely Eric's mother Catherine and her sister Deborah who was also known as Debby, were allocated the large bedroom next door to Robyn's room. Eric being the only man on the delegation, already swollen headed by having been appointed leader of the delegation by Lawyer James Q-T thought he would be allocated the airy corner master bedroom but unfortunately that was a composite part of the house which would remain locked by custom until after the rites for which they made the trip had been performed. When Eric's secret wish of occupying his late uncle's master bedroom was shattered by strict application of the traditional rules, he was about to protest when the caretaker informed the whole retinue that he was acting strictly to instructions dictated by the head of their family. Apart from the master bedroom suite and the adjacent two bedrooms just allocated to the ladies of the delegation,

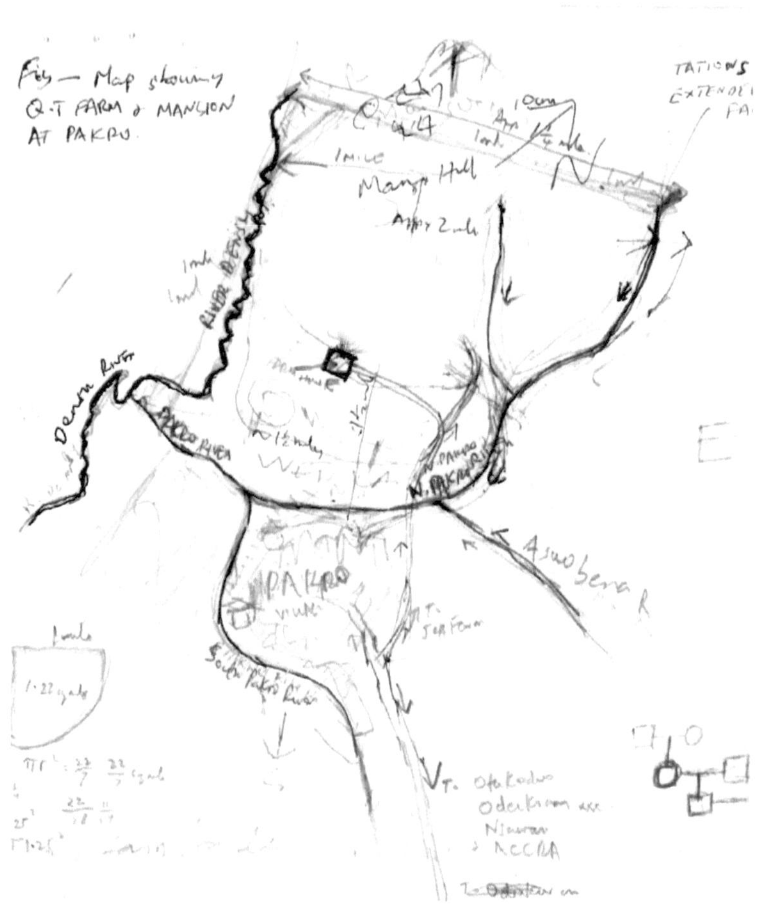

Map showing Q-T farm and mansion at Pakro

there were no other rooms at this south-west wing of this large mansion. Next to the third bedroom allocated to the two elderly ladies was a narrow passage perpendicular to the main corridor on the north side of the main bedrooms referred to above. The main corridor then continued in an easterly direction with several rooms lined up along it to the east end of the block. The passage adjacent to the third bedroom crossed the main east-west corridor at right angles and continued northwards for 20 yards fully roofed and walled on both sides except for two large windows in the western wall and a wide door in the eastern wall leading into an inner courtyard. The roofed passage led to a cluster of flat roofed structures which served as stores and kitchens at the east end and bath house at the west end. Directly behind and to the north of the bathhouse were situated the well-constructed toilets securely gated and roofed. Beyond and further east of the large indoor/outdoor kitchen was a security wall with a gate forming the eastern limit of the inner courtyard.

Situated at the south east corner of the inner courtyard and next to the main entrance were the foyer, lounge and dining areas of the farm mansion. The open space to the east of the wall served as the outer courtyard to the north of which were a long line of structures which housed the servants, workers etc. The apartment of the farm managers and their families were clustered in this area. The main road to the estate lay in front of the servant's quarters, while to the south of the road and south-west of the mansion for several hectares all the way to the bend of the big Densu river where it is joined by the Pakro stream marking the southwest corner stretched the magnificent flat undulating southern portion of the farm of the late Jeffrey Quinton Taki. This portion of the farm was criss-crossed by slow flowing streams and rivulets which were all functional un-mapped tributaries of the Pakro river to the south and the

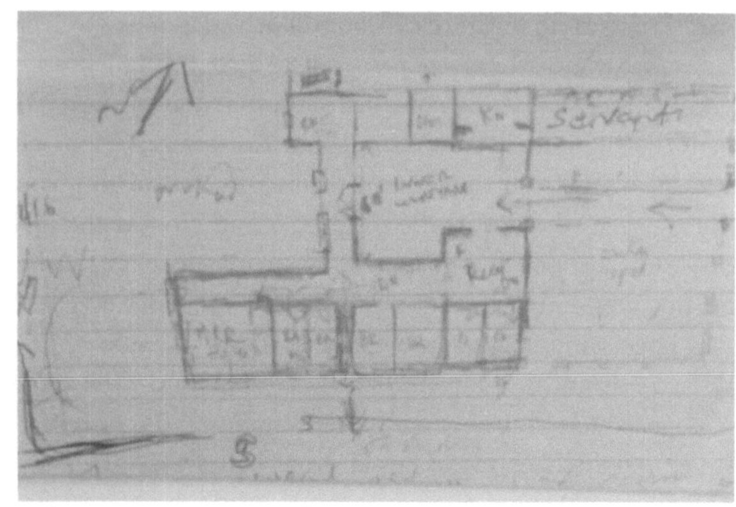

Floor plan of Q.T Farmhouse

The farmhouse at Pakro

Densu river to the west. The southern border of the land was the Pakro river from its point of entry into the Densu river in the southwest to where its tributary the Asuobena river joined the Pakro river at the south east corner of the plot.

There were several medium sized rooms along the main corridor which had never been used as the house, built with a large family in mind, never had in residence a devoted wife prepared or able to bear and bring up several children. The unfortunate tragedy which was the cause of this anomaly occurred when Robyn was only six years old. The head of the extended family, not happy with his wife's inability to produce more children nagged her to the point where she had to leave unceremoniously never to be seen nor heard of again. There were several rumours, but the truth emerged after several years. A subordinate clerk of the household had apparently eloped with her and they were spotted living together in the Northern territories, she still childless while her rival the second 'wife' of her lover had produced several children. It then became obvious that the difficult childbirth of her first and only daughter Robyn, which event was associated with loss of too much blood had led to sterility. Farmer Jeff never married again, but rather chose to remain single and devote all his time and energy to looking after the farm and bringing up his only daughter.

When Jeff died, the family decided that for security reasons the loyal caretaker should move into the last two end rooms at the east end of the main house in order to keep a close eye on the property. James as head of family volunteered to visit the farm periodically to ensure the continuation of the business until Robyn became an adult and took over with her husband as stated in Jeff's last will and testament. During the past six months and since the death of Farmer Jeff, Collins the caretaker had *grown wings* in the community, being the only well-educated man apart from the couple of village schoolteachers and the local UAC agent. He had expanded his family property and farms, acquired a wedded wife and started a family. He therefore hardly lived at the Jeff farm which was three miles from Pakro town. Collins's two room well furnished apartment at the east end of the main corridor was what was allocated to Eric on this visit, and he liked it very much and decided that he would try to keep it as a permanent country home subject to family approval.

The welcoming get-together with the sumptuous dinner and drinks ended at about 9.00 pm and the villagers departed in a joyous mood leaving the visitors and the farm security at their posts far away from the farmhouse itself. The farm dogs, the backbone of farm security, were released and all was suddenly so peaceful and quiet that apart from the branches whistling in obedience to the wind and the occasional barking of nocturnal animals, the silence was absolute. For the city folk the contrast with the noisy sounds of the city was awe inspiring. As soon as the villagers left the servants retired to their quarters, the main gate was shut and bolted from inside and the four visitors from the city retired from the courtyard into the mansion. They relaxed in comfortable armchairs for small talk. Eric remembered that they had refused the drink offered by the villagers. He announced that he suspected that they were all thirsty and in need of wholesome fluid. Head of family Q-T had made sure that cartons of imported beer and lemonade had accompanied them on the blind side of the ladies. Eric was the only one who had prior knowledge of this -- the elderly ladies and the young lady as well were pleasantly surprised. Eric offered beer to the ladies and lemonade to Robyn. He decided to join them for beer although he had smuggled in a bottle of fine brandy when James was packing the drinks.

Village party

Village Drummers

Robyn was tasked to rinse and wipe the glasses with a clean napkin and, while she was at it, Eric joined her to offer her a helping hand and moral support. He advised her not to touch the beer because it was supposed to send the elderly ladies to bed early so the young ones could continue the party deep into the night. Robyn looked at him and flirted brazenly telling him that she knew what he was trying to do. Eric agreed that the whole exercise smacked of an irresistible temptation which he hoped was mutual. Robyn just sighed and continued her little chore.

Eric had stacked the beer in earthenware pots containing cold water. The walls of the pots being permeable allowed water to seep from the inside across the porous clay on to the surface: evaporation of the film of this surface water extracted latent heat from the water inside and cooled it in the process. The beer was therefore nicely chilled when it was served to the old ladies and they enjoyed it thoroughly. The long journey under the heat of the day plus the early evening village reception and heavy meal had rendered all of them tired and dehydrated. When the cool drinks became available thirst became more obvious and they virtually gulped down the first two glasses within minutes. Eric encouraged them by doing same. He was used to drinking several bottles of beer on nights with good company at the Sekondi club therefore he was sure that two or three glasses would not affect his senses as much they would affect and indeed dull the senses of the old ladies who custom demanded to drink beer infrequently and in small quantities. The trick worked; after the initial excitement and animated free talk and gossip, the old ladies became drowsy and started dosing off obviously. Robyn suggested to her aunts that they would be more comfortable sleeping in their own beds. They agreed and Robyn held them both and led them gingerly along the long corridor to their room. Within minutes of changing

Marriage-salvaging meeting at Cape Coast

into their night gowns and climbing into the bedstead the two ladies fell into a deep slumber. Robyn shut their door and went to her own room where she also changed into her night gown and laid on her bed, but sleep did not come to her so easily partly because she was young and strong and the day's activities had not affected her that much, but more importantly she had not touched the beer which was obviously working as a sedative on her elderly relatives. She knew what the plans had been concocted for and she knew he was waiting for her to come to him. She resisted the temptation to go to Eric with all her moral strength, but her effort was in vain because the temptation was irresistible. She got out of bed, put on her sandals, opened the door and stepped into the long quiet corridor. After three or four steps she was at the door of the guest room where her elderly aunts were asleep the last time she saw them. She opened the door without knocking and the squeak of the hinges made her cringe. She stepped gently to their bedside and there she heard the gentle snore from one of them, the final proof that they were fast asleep, and the beer had worked as sedative. She decided to test the situation one last time before she made her final move by banging the nearby dressing table hard with a wooden hairbrush twice. The loud noise failed totally to stir the old ladies who remained fast asleep and still snoring. She decided to take her chance now that she had well and truly yielded to temptation. She shut the door of the old ladies' room gently and hurried along the long corridor towards Eric's room. She reckoned the time was approximately 10.30 pm and the whole estate was dark, and all the servants were fast asleep. She also knew that some of the servants were notorious for snooping around looking for gossip. She looked all around and listened carefully for human sounds; when she was sure that there were no spies, she rushed quickly across the hall, opened the door gently without a creak. The room was dark, but she could see the white bed sheet illuminated by the soft moonlight coming through the jalousies of the closed window. She knew that Eric had already seen her because she heard his enhanced heavy breathing which made her likewise start breathing heavily.

It had been 45 minutes since the get together with the old ladies ended and they sauntered back leaving Eric alone in his apartment, Robyn was therefore surprised to note that he had done nothing since. He was still fully dressed and had drunk nothing. The bottle of brandy which he had reserved for himself remained uncorked and he was perched uncomfortably on the side of the bed with his shoe-clad feet firmly on the floor.

He whispered with an obvious sigh, “I have been expecting you every minute! I am mighty glad you have come at last; I would have come to you but it was too risky. Well done!”

Robyn replied: “I suspected that you were waiting for me, but I had to make sure that my aunts were fast asleep before I ventured such a delicate manoeuvre.”

Eric responded thus, “I have been waiting for the opportunity to be alone with you all week, and sometimes your secret, quiet flirtations when no one was looking in our direction drove me beyond limits, and I thought those temptations without opportunities for action were just teases to drive me crazy.”

Robyn was happy the feelings were mutual and at that instance threw herself into his arms with utmost abandon. She was wearing only a light-weight knee-length gown and therefore he encountered her full body with all the voluptuous curves of a precocious 17-year-old girl against his body and the feeling was exhilarating. She had developed substantially since they first met, her breasts had become bigger and fuller but still very firm, her nipples had become dark brown almost black pebbles springy and rough on their plateaus, and her rear equally round and protuberant were inviting and just amazing to touch and caress. She grew weaker in the legs as the fondling of her body persisted to the point when she could not control herself any more so that she fell backwards on the bed at the same time pulling him on top of her belly. He was by then fully aroused, he therefore started removing his clothes frantically, that was the signal for her to pull her flimsy night gown over her head thus rendering herself fully naked. He grabbed and pressed her sweaty, warm and excited body to his. She wriggled her body instinctively so that his lower trunk lay between her firm, long shapely thighs, crotch against crotch. They were both ready for the consummation which followed naturally and rhythmically but slowly at first then rising through a prolonged powerful crescendo resulting in a perfect mutual satisfaction. Although they both yearned for a period of rest in each other's arms for recovery and repetition, they felt that time was not on their side and that Robyn must hurry to her room without delay before her aunts woke up and started looking for her. She jumped out of the bed, put on her night gown, pecked Eric on the cheek, hurriedly unlocked the door and crept noiselessly out of the room and onto the long corridor. There were no noises or movements anywhere and she was reassured that their recent adventure or misadventure was a secret. She went past the door of her aunts' room without attempting to open it; reached the door of her own room which she opened gently. The room was quite dark, but she dared not put on the lantern. She removed her sweat-soaked night gown and towelled her body dry with a fresh towel, changed into her spare night gown. She was then ready to go and see what had happened to her aunts. She opened their door quietly and sighed deeply when she heard the same snoring noises she heard prior to leaving their side two hours ago. She crept gently to their bedside to reassure herself that they were both fast asleep. On observing that they were both still fast asleep, she retreated to the door, crept out onto the corridor and re-entered her room. No sooner had she laid supine on her bed than she started daydreaming about what had just taken place between her and Eric.

The daydreaming was very pleasant, and she resolved that the reality must be repeated sooner than later. On second thoughts she changed her mind reckoning that it was too risky and must not be repeated when the area was obviously crawling with servants and labourers; grown up men and women whom she knew had great propensity for spying and gossiping about their masters and madams. Henceforth at least while they were in the village and farm, on no account must she look or even glance in the direction of Eric because she feared she might betray her true feelings such that a nosy and observant bystander might suspect that there existed a romantic relationship between her and Eric. She loved Eric with all her heart; no, it was not infatuation! It was true love, and she was sure that Eric also loved her with all his heart and she prayed that nothing should happen to endanger this mutual feeling which should last forever. She lay on her bed for several hours fully awake while the earlier excitement rather lingered on stubbornly. Sleep finally came deeply and accompanied by pleasant romantic dreams, but it was short lived.

She was rudely awakened by a knock on her door. Before she responded, she begged the good Lord that it would not be Eric. She voiced out a feeble "Come in, the door is not locked."

She was greatly relieved when Maame Esi the elderly chief female servant who had been briefed by the chief overseer to look after them walked into her chamber. She then realised that dawn had broken as soft rays of the early morning sun were already peeping through the jalousies of the window. Maame Esi politely informed her that water for her bath was ready in the bath house and she must hurry to go and take her bath and then come and help her aunts to go and do same. She also informed her that breakfast was being prepared and that the overseer and her cousin Eric had gone for a long drive to the oil palm plantation which was about two miles away and finally that she was expecting them for breakfast in about an hour. It would not be polite if they ate alone without the company of the ladies. Robyn agreed and rushed to the bath house. She had a quick bath, returned to her room, changed into decent house clothes then went to her aunts' room. They were awake chatting and were happy to see her. She told them her mission and they all rushed to the bath house.

The timing was perfect in that Robyn and her aunts arrived at the hall where breakfast had been laid out just when Eric and the overseer returned from their walk in Wellington boots and dark green khaki trousers.

Breakfast was a buffet, and the items covered a very wide range of typical Ga morning dishes namely, ekuegbeemli, aboboi ke tatale, oblayoo, akasa or koko, komi ke kenan/loo ni asha, etc. After breakfast Eric's mother now the substantive matriarch of the family and head of the small delegation to Pakro and Jeff's farms announced that the next item was the main business of the trip namely the one-year ceremony of opening and entering the private chamber and inspecting the personal effects and private documents of their departed brother, father and uncle. Since the pending ceremony was by custom restricted to close family members only, the caretaker was politely asked to leave to attend to other duties. The family members consisting of the matriarch Catherine, her sister Debby, their son and nephew Eric and last but not the least Robyn the daughter of the deceased brother of Catherine and Debby. They all stood in front of the locked door of the bedroom suite of the late Jeff Quinton-Taki. Traditional prayers were said after the

Touring Pakro Farms in horse-driven cart

Christian prayers by Catherine. The key was then pulled out of Catherine's bag by Robyn and handed over to Eric the only man on the delegation. Eric symbolically knocked on the door three times. When there was no response, he was requested by Catherine to open the door fully prepared symbolically to face and overcome all unforeseen dangers before the ladies attempted to enter. He did just that and they all entered the room which had truly not been entered since Jeff died. The room was dark but after a couple of minutes their eyes adjusted and they were able to see the bed, wardrobes, tables, desks, chairs exactly as they were left by the deceased. The windows were opened by Eric, letting in more light. The room was dusty and full of cobwebs, evidence that no humans had entered the room for a long time. Catherine was pleased that the custom had been strictly adhered to and therefore Jeff's spirit was at peace to bless all his living relatives.

They opened the wardrobes, chest of drawers and boxes and laid bare all his worldly possessions. They then went to his desk and saw that all papers and documents were there and undisturbed. They could tell by the pattern of dust on the surface of these items. Eric then noticed that there was a metal safe standing at the far corner at the other side of the bed and against the wall. The heavy metal door was locked. Robyn announced that the key was in her possession at the time of her father's death. Father himself gave it to her for safe keeping and advised her to give it to no one other than her uncle the lawyer. She did that and her uncle had returned it to her to keep until that very moment.

She gave the key to her aunt Catherine who in turn gave it to Eric. Eric opened the door. The contents surprised them all. Jeff obviously did not trust the banks. The safe contained a lot of cash, documents of the property, deeds and signed indentures from the chiefs from whom he acquired this vast piece of land several years ago, and receipts of all payments he had made over the years. Jeff had written a will witnessed by his brother lawyer James Q-T, in which he had bequeathed three-quarters of all his worldly possessions to his only daughter effective when she turned 21. Before then James Q-T was to be Robyn's guardian and custodian of her inheritance. According to the will, the remaining quarter of the estate was to go to the extended family and that too was to be administered by lawyer James Q-T. Now that the contents of the safe were known, albeit by close family members only, they thought it was unsafe to let it remain in the room.

They decided to carry it to Accra on their return trip. The documents on his desk and drawers would also go to Accra. The jewellery, paraphernalia, and valuable kente cloths were too bulky to accompany them. Custom demanded those who had performed the ceremony to dip their hands into the residue and items of their choice and keep them as souvenirs to remind them of the occasion forever which they all did. They packed the stuff into the wardrobes and locked the door. The keys were secured in a safe bag and handed over to Catherine and they were quickly out of the place before strangers who were probably lurking around could come close enough to eavesdrop on their private proceedings.

They planned their return journey and decided to depart early the next morning for which purpose they sent messengers to the carriage driver in Pakro village to prepare the vehicle for the journey back to Accra.

RETURN JOURNEY TO ACCRA

The safe was very heavy, but the enlisted helpers rounded up at the last minute managed to load it on the cart. Eric had taken care of security and arranged for policemen to accompany them on the journey to Accra. They set off at about 6.00 am when the sun was just rearing its head above the eastern horizon. It was a cool morning and there was a gentle breeze from the south east. The gravel road having been well watered by a gentle rain which had fallen the previous night was free of dust. Soon they were rolling along the main road of Pakro heading rapidly past thatched-roofed and few sandcrete buildings with zinc roofs on either side of the main street. The landscape suddenly changed, and they were hobbling along in the thick tropical rain forest of the Eastern province of the Gold Coast colony towards the next big town called Kwakyekrom by the indigenous people. There they stopped for breakfast of koko and oven fresh bread. It was obviously getting warmer; but as soon they left town, they encountered the cool forest/tree canopied pleasant atmosphere. The traffic was sparse and quiet and there were only few travellers on foot and accompanied by their stout porters carrying heavy loads on their heads doing the long journey probably all the way to Accra. They were happy to see them because they provided security for the treasure in old Jeff's safe which they were praying would arrive in Accra safely to be handed over to lawyer James Q-T. The rest of the journey to Accra was uneventful except that they had to stop in several villages to enable the ladies to buy a variety of items and farm fresh foodstuff, while the driver and his mates watered or changed horses. As soon as they arrived at Nsawam the busy cosmopolitan market town they felt they were back to civilisation. Well-dressed men were visible everywhere minding their own business. The roads were broader and not so bumpy enabling the vehicle to run relatively smoothly. They resisted

Men pushing barrel containers on wheels on the road to Pakro

the temptation to stop at Nsawam because they wanted to reach Accra before nightfall.

They finally came to the end of the tiring journey when they entered the gates of Q-T mansions and the carriage rolled noisily along the gravel lane from the gate to the porch. Lawyer James was sitting at the porch waiting anxiously for them and as soon as the carriage came to a halt, he jumped on to his feet to welcome his sisters, nephew Eric and niece Robyn whom he suspected had gone through an emotional turmoil. House servants were called to help carry the safe upstairs into the master bedroom, and the travellers trooped upstairs into the sanctum to tell their stories and revelations to the patriarch.

He listened with rapt attention without interfering with the narration. When the ceremonial leader of the delegation

Catherine finished speaking lawyer James thanked her and her fellow delegates profusely and asked if any of them had anything to say. When none of them obliged he asked the youngest of them Robyn how she felt. She naturally broke down crying while her elderly aunt embraced and consoled her affectionately. As custom demanded the safe was opened in the presence of all, and a detailed inventory was taken witnessed and signed by all including the beneficiary, Robyn.

Patriarch James promised to study the documents thoroughly during the course of the week and report back. He also told them that he would open a special account at Bank of British West Africa in town and deposit for safe keeping all the cash and valuables found that day in his late brother's safe. They all agreed that Jeff had done well in life and died a rich man. A short prayer was said by Catherine and the formal meeting was brought to a close. The long day ended with a late dinner at 8.00 pm and by 9.00 pm they had all gone to bed since the next day was a full working day. How they had all wished that it was the weekend so frolicking, and celebrations could have gone on endlessly. But alas! It was not so, and they accepted their fate graciously.

The next morning for lawyer James was business as usual. He and his wife got up early and took their baths. The lawyer put on his working clothes, had a quick breakfast and was out of the house by 7.30 am. He arrived at the High Court at 8.30 am and had 30 minutes to ponder over his pending case but before then he thought deeply about the previous day's affairs and wondered why his sister did not discuss the possibility of Eric taking over the management of Jeff Farms and business at Pakro. He had briefed her on the subject, and they had agreed and hoped that Eric, on seeing the vastness and potential of the place would be tempted to at least part ownership. He specifically asked his sister to talk to her son about it, but so far they had both remained silent on the issue. He decided that after completing his duties at the High Court he would go straight to his sister's place and have a one-on-one straight talk with her.

Lawyer James arrived at his sister's house at 1.00 pm and he was welcomed warmly by his sister Kate.

She asked with a broad smile, "What brings you to my humble abode without any prior warning? I hope it is not devastating bad news."

"It is urgent business alright, but not a tragedy at all, although it could turn so if we do not act fast to prevent a possible catastrophe."

"Brother! You are frightening me. What is the big problem on your mind?"

"Sister I did not sleep a wink last night because you were absolutely silent on the strategy to talk to Eric at Pakro about the possibility of taking over Jeff Farms."

Kate took in a deep breath and said, "I did, and found that he was not interested, he was not at all impressed by the property neither was he tempted by the immense potential wealth the estate represented. He thought the entire enterprise belonged to Robyn, and that the caretaker must continue running it, while you continued to supervise it until Robyn's 21st birthday when Jeff's will was due to mature."

"You have disappointed me immensely by your inability to communicate to your son what I think should be a real temptation to any young man."

"Honestly, I did communicate with him, and even told him

that if he did not yield to the temptation, an asset which truly belongs to the family would end up in the hands of strangers. He disagreed and insisted that the young lady inheritor will marry one day and produce children specifically Jeff's grand and great grandchildren to whom the fruits of his labours really belonged."

James being aware that he was losing the current argument tactfully retreated saying, "I will rush home, have a quick lunch and talk to Eric."

James was true to his word. Lunch was ready when he arrived so he invited Eric to lunch and told him that they would have an important conversation in the library after lunch. After lunch, James and his nephew Eric left Mrs Q-T to her own devices and went to the library. James started the conversation: "The trip to Pakro and Jeff's farm was meant to accomplish several things, I hope you realised that."

"Yes, of course, and they were accomplished."

"No, they were not. The ceremonial re-entry of Jeff's room and the inspection of his worldly possessions and documents were only two of them. The most important was to deliberate on the continuing running of the farm and who was to take over the business, and I had advised your mother to brief you on site after you had a look at the estate, but alas! Since you returned neither of you have volunteered any statement. I have just come from your mother's house, and quite honestly I did not like what I managed to extract from her, I want to know your own opinion."

"Well uncle we had long talks, sometimes bordering on heated arguments. I made myself quite clear that I was not prepared to quit my thriving business at Sekondi, my 18 months marriage blessed already with a baby boy and take up a plantation business about which I know next to nothing."

"Never mind knowing nothing now; you will learn fast, after all you are a Q-T and a brilliant one at that."

"Well uncle, this time round the Wuta gene has taken the upper hand and the quiet office routine trait has taken a good hold of me. The shipping business in Sekondi is good, I have made some good new friends there, and I am enjoying the family life."

James, realizing that his nephew was stubborn, threw in his trump card.

"Just think and remember that the whole estate will be yours for the taking if you marry Robyn."

Eric retorted without hesitation, "That is impossible! Indeed, I am quite shocked hearing you of all people say that; is it not considered a taboo marrying a close relative, have you forgotten that she and I are first cousins?"

"No, in our tradition it is not this way round, the parents of the two of you namely your mother and Robyn's father Jeff are brother and sister alright, but she being the man's daughter and you the woman's (Kate's) son, you are allowed to marry, it is not a taboo. The other way round is frowned upon and can be embarrassing for several reasons including the surname of the possible offspring. This way round your children will bear your surname Wuta and it will not be obvious that you are related."

Eric argued, "It is not the surname which matters, the phenomenon is a taboo whether it is this way or the other way round, and I read that it is considered a crime in certain European countries. When it was practised in series among the Pharaohs of Egypt their offspring became feeble minded to extinction. Likewise, European royal families who married their cousins produced very sick children and they managed to remedy the situation by every now and then injecting exotic Asiatic, Oriental or even Negroid royalty for hybrid vigour. The important thing is that even in our native circles, it is a taboo for close relatives to co-habit, it happens but always in secret."

"Eric, when it is convenient and expedient as it is now, we have a duty to try it. Do you not like your beautiful cousin? her height matches yours perfectly and you will command a stunning presence dressed up and out at a ball."

"I now understand why you are such a successful lawyer; you have what in business and sports we call the killer instinct of champions. But if you feel so strongly about the expediency, why don't you consider your own proposition?"

The lawyer in James enabled him to maintain a civilised composure despite the near insolent argument from his own favourite nephew; he responded calmly thus:

"I cannot because my children are near her age and she is my daughter. For you she is a younger sister and a friend."

"Uncle, this conversation is really heavy, and I hope no one is eavesdropping."

"Let them eavesdrop. It will awaken them to know about human nature and propel them to maturity."

"Uncle, I will take leave now and go and lie down in bed and think about these rather complex issues. By the way there is a boat leaving for Sekondi on Thursday and I plan to be on it. Thank you for a lively conversation. I have not agreed with your proposal but as I said I will continue to think about it."

This hot jungle of emotions took over his mind completely as he rested alone in his room hoping that nobody not even his treasure Robyn came to disturb him. He fell asleep and when he woke up it was dusk and the whole mansion was quiet. One of the maidservants came and knocked on his door to announce that dinner was ready. He was tempted to waive dinner but in this Quinton-Taki household that action would cause a revolution so he decided to brave it and go to dinner. Dinner was pleasant and uneventful, and he managed to join the small talk during which he mentioned his impending departure. That did not cause much of a surprise because the rumour had already done the rounds.

Dinner was over by 7.30 pm. Mr and Mrs Q-T were due to go to a wake-keeping, so they went to their room to prepare while Eric went straight to bed hoping to continue his quiet meditation and preparations for his trip to Sekondi on the morrow to comfort his dear wife and reunite with his new baby boy whom he had missed badly during these past few weeks in Accra. He soon felt sleepy and dozed off into a deep slumber. The house was very quiet that night and everything felt peaceful. He had lost the sense of time when in the distance he heard a soft knock on his door which creaked open. He remembered that he forgot to lock the door as he had planned. He knew instinctively that it was Robyn who had entered his room. She came to the side of his bed and whispered, "Are you awake?"

He answered, "Yes Robyn, but it is dangerous to walk in here at this time, we will certainly be caught red handed and there will be a scandal."

Robyn retorted, "What scandal? There will be no scandal. By the way I eavesdropped on your conversation with my uncle this afternoon and heard clearly that it was his strategic wish that the two of us should marry each other despite our being first cousins in order to keep the vast property within the family and safely beyond the reach of strangers. Anyway, the children are fast asleep, and uncle and auntie have gone to a wake keeping in town and not expected back until well after midnight. It is now only 9.30 pm, darling, we have plenty of time, everything is under control, even the servants have been persuaded to stay far away from the main house."

Eric said nothing but secretly admired the ingenuity of his beautiful young cousin.

"Eric! Were you planning to leave Accra to-morrow morning without saying an intimate goodbye? You should know by now that I love you."

"My dear Robyn, I love you too, but remember I am married under the ordinance to a wife who has just delivered my second son."

"Never mind all that, we have only one life so let us live to the full whatever our fate fashions out for us."

Robyn then boldly joined her love in bed and they embraced, fondled and kissed each other warmly and passionately for a long time before they finally consummated their love to a hot and uninhibited climax. After lying in each other's arms for several minutes they suddenly came their senses and became aware of the peculiar if not precarious circumstances under which they were operating, especially the possibility of being caught red-handed by their elderly relatives. They stopped abruptly, Robyn jumped out of the bed, said a hurried goodbye and rushed out of the room.

In the morning Eric had to leave early before breakfast in order to catch the speed boat to Sekondi. He looked back from the gate when the carriage on which he was travelling was about to exit the compound and he saw Robyn in the distance standing at the front porch of the mansion. He waved to her and she waved back smiling.

BACK TO SEKONDI

He was welcomed at Sekondi port by the usual crowd including his wife and baby and he almost enjoyed the situation. Sekondi was always carefree and unconventional as far as he was concerned. Of late Accra life for him had become exotic and complicated. Robyn was always on his mind on sight therefore he could not concentrate on serious matters. On the other hand, at Sekondi, he had important duties to perform both at home and at the workplace. However, old habits die hard, so it was not surprising that he drifted to the club in the evening, and he was glad he went. The atmosphere was charged, everybody was there and eager to hear what had transpired in Accra. Snippets of news had sneaked in via occasional travellers but all and sundry wished to hear the authentic story from the horse's

Robyn waves goodbye to Eric on his way to Accra Port bound for Sekondi

own mouth. Charged with a couple of beers and inspired by lively atmosphere, Eric over-reached himself and was at his conversational best. He was amazed that he could remember minute details of all events especially those involving the numerous receptions including the imperial rituals imported from London.

At home he was the best of husbands, seizing every opportunity to dote on his wife and new son who obviously resembled him despite the baby features. He tried hard to forget the recent events of Accra especially his intimate affairs with Robyn by focussing on his wife, family life and his business which was doing very well thanks to his loyal and efficient chief clerk.

THE TELEGRAM FROM ACCRA

Daily and weekly life for Eric in Sekondi remained gentle and predictable for several weeks except for periods when Robyn came up in his daydreams. On those occasions he wondered what she was doing and genuinely missed her company. He noticed that this time round she had refused to write to him, and he knew the reason. He behaved abominably in the past by failing to reply to her numerous letters. The shipping, warehousing and retailing businesses were all flourishing, and he was getting richer literally by the hour. He was convinced he had taken the correct decision when he resisted the temptation so tactfully presented by his clever uncle who nearly convinced him to give up Sekondi for Jeff's farms at Pakro. He also continued to enjoy social life especially the visits to the club, the weekend parties and the Sunday morning church services at the Sekondi Wesley Cathedral where he always enjoyed singing the inspiring and tuneful Methodist hymns. All the elements of peaceful good life enumerated above ended abruptly that afternoon when news arrived per a private courier from Lawyer James Quinton-Taki. It came in the form of a special and confidential telegram carrying a secret message meant for the attention of the addressee only. Eric received the sealed envelope in his office where the courier had been asked to deliver the telegram with further instructions that on no account must anybody including Eric's wife know of the delivery. Since he did not want the courier to observe his reaction, he tipped and dismissed him before he opened the sealed envelope. He had a premonition that the message was important or delicate, he therefore locked the office door before he tore open the several layers of envelopes to finally reach the note from his uncle. The note was brief and to the point. *"Robyn is three months pregnant, and she has named you Eric Wuta as responsible for the pregnancy. Kindly rush to Accra without delay to help us sort things out and know the way forward."* It was signed James Q-T.

It dawned on him there and then that three and half months had rapidly gone by since he returned to Sekondi from Accra and by a quick calculation he reckoned that it was the reckless and careless union with Robyn in the village which led to the pregnancy. Hitherto he had prided himself to having mastered the technique of withdrawal at the crucial moment, and he had used the technique to avoid impregnating several women during the time he was at the height of womanisation. He recalled on that infamous night he was drunk and was carried away by the raw passion he felt for Robyn. The worst had happened, the scandal was already at hand and he must go to Accra immediately for the process of reparation to begin.

He checked the boat departure schedule and luckily a slow boat was due to leave the next morning for Accra. It was one of those which stopped at every landing on the way, but it was better than nothing. At home that afternoon, he announced that a business emergency had come up and he had to rush to Accra the following morning. It was going to be a short turn around trip, and he would be back in 5 days. The poor wife was reticent because she sensed it was a fait accompli. She helped him pack a few things and first thing in the morning without even bothering to have breakfast he rushed to Sekondi port to catch the mail boat which was due to depart at 6.00 am. The voyage was uneventful, and the boat arrived safely at Accra port on schedule at 5.30 pm. After disembarkation, he rushed to his uncle's mansion at Tudu and found that the elders had gathered and were waiting for him on the veranda. Traditional greetings were said, and he was given water to drink. Papa lawyer Q-T was the first to speak.

"The post boy early this morning delivered a Morse code telegram which alerted us that you had departed from Sekondi at 6.00 am and will arrive in Accra in the late afternoon. Recognizing the importance and urgency of this meeting and above all your prompt response to our request we decided to assemble and wait for you."

It was Eric's turn to speak and he went straight to the point. "I received your message via courier three days ago at mid-day, and since you do not routinely use that method of communication I was frightened and therefore opened the package with trepidation after ensuring that I was alone in my office with the door securely locked. I must say I took in a deep breath of relief when I read the message."

Eric's mother barged in angrily, "So you thought it was not important eh! Eric, how insensitive you have become?"

"Please, please, please," interjected Q-T, "…all he meant was that he was relieved it was not a terrible tragedy."

Eric then said, "Mother I am really sorry to have upset you by my opening remarks, I should have been more circumspect. After reading the urgent message, I arranged an urgent passage and by the grace of God I have arrived safely."

Eric's uncle the learned lawyer diffused the tension by saying; "You have travelled a great distance, and tradition demands that you should speak first, especially as you have come in response to an urgent message, so we are all ears."

Eric started with a polite question: "By the way where is Robyn and is she well?"

His mother replied "She is fine and now lives with me in town. We thought that was more appropriate because of her condition."

"Thank you, mother, all that Robyn has told you is the truth. I am responsible for her present condition and accept all duties attached."

Eric's mother waded in angrily again, "Eric how could you do that? How long has this been going on anyway?"

"Since we first met during my visit a year ago in this house."

"What about the current pregnancy, when was the union?"

"It was at Pakro 3 to 4 months ago."

"Eric! You mean you had no respect for our serious assignment at Pakro and rather took advantage of the situation to perpetrate such an act."

"Please mother, I did not take advantage of our important assignment, as I said earlier, it started over a year ago. I love her and I believe she loves me too. I am ready and willing to do all that is necessary. If I may recall that when we discussed the issue at Pakro you said that although we were first cousins, in other words children of a brother and sister) the daughter of the brother was allowed to marry the son of the sister, the other way round you said was problematic."

"That offer was refused by you and you invoked the serious consequences of consanguineous marriages to win the argument. You deceived me badly because you had already or about to consummate a consanguineous union."

Elder Q-T was the next to speak. "The girl is already pregnant therefore the important business is how to manage the situation and its social consequences. She is nearly four months pregnant therefore the question of abortion does not come in. Our aim is to protect the lives of Robyn and the unborn one who is also our flesh and blood. Since Eric has accepted responsibility, he is going to give the expected one a name: to begin with the surname will be Wuta. The third problem concerns the status of Robyn. Will she remain an unmarried mother or not? At this point let me step aside and pursue purely the duty of a Quintin-Taki and put an important question to mother and son. What will be the status of my daughter Robyn? I pause for an answer."

Kate was quick with the appropriate response as follows: "Brother remember that I am also a Quintin-Taki. My late husband in other words Eric's late father died several years ago but he left behind living relatives to be consulted on family issues. Let us leave that option to Eric himself who is a fully grown adult capable of handling his own affairs."

"I agree with mother, just give me a few hours to think and I will give you an answer."

That brought a surprisingly civilized discussion to an end for the mean time. Considering the complexity of the situation they recognised and commended each other for their mutual tolerance.

After that short meeting, Eric's mother suggested that he should accompany her to her house to visit Robyn and for some private talk as suggested by his uncle. Before they left the Q-T mansions, she engaged him in a long chat at the far corner of the veranda to make sure that there were no eavesdroppers. She also wanted privacy from even Robyn whom she knew had sharp ears just like her late father Jeff. She started their private conversation by asking Eric whether he was well acquainted with the traditional rules which his uncle had referred to as regards Robyn's pregnancy. Eric affirmed that he knew the fact that a man who admits to impregnating a woman out of wedlock was obliged by traditional rules to look after the woman during the pregnancy, pay for her upkeep including rent, food, and medical expenses up to and including delivery expenses and looking after the child until he or she became an adult capable of self-sustenance. Mother commended son on his knowledge but added that he had left out a few things.

"Your uncle is very wise, with a shrewd legal mind. The challenge he has thrown to us derives from traditional custom which maintains that he should also be prepared to name the child which implies that the new-born will bear his family name or surname in addition to any other name which the father of the child wanted to give. No one has the right to name the child except the man who has owned up by offering drinks that signified that indeed he is responsible for the pregnancy all other challengers well confounded. The real problem is what happens to the mother after the delivery. The principle is that nobody must marry under duress, no one must be coerced to marry because of pregnancy. Marriage must be clearly separated from accidental or incidental pregnancy. Once the baby is born the two parties are free to go their separate ways and must not be forced to get married. Eric, remember you are already married with two sons, the first aged two years and the second less than a year old. Your uncle wants you to think carefully in order to take a good decision. If I may ask the first question; do you love Robyn or was it just lust?"

Eric took in a deep breath and answered in the affirmative.

"Your answer does not surprise me because I have already talked to Robyn at length, and she also confessed that she loves you. The second question, your mutual love not withstanding is do you wish to marry her, bearing in mind that you are already married under the ordinance and taking another wife will be bigamy as far as the church and European laws are concerned. If you marry a second wife, you will be excommunicated and indeed you will lose your standing as a church goer. Nobody can stop you from calling yourself a Christian or going to church, but the clergy and elders of the church will distance themselves from you and you will not hold any church society office or position. The Europeans cannot do you much harm because you have no intention of living in Europe with two wives; however if you do, they will charge you with bigamy and imprison you, it has happened before. Before you answer this complicated question, I think you must discuss the issue with Robyn. If the two of you wish to marry then you Eric in particular must consider the last but not the least problem which is how you will manage your current wife and sons in such a situation, and finally how you will break the news to your wife before some stranger does. Fortunately, you have six months to think. The question of whether to marry Robyn will become crucial after the delivery in six months, till then nobody apart from those who already know about the pregnancy need to be informed. When the baby arrives the naming ceremony will be announced and performed. I would like you to delay your final answer to me and your uncle until you have had a good chat with Robyn. Let us now go to my house and meet her".

They arrived at Mrs Wuta's small town house at about 9.00 pm. The house was the marital house when her husband was alive and now she owned the house fully, thanks to her late husband who bequeathed it to her in his will. Thanks also were due to her clever brother and lawyer who succeeded to brush aside all challengers from the Wuta extended family who tried to evict her. She lived there with her only son Eric until he moved to Sekondi two years ago.

She was an expert seamstress and her home doubled as her business centre and famous vocational institute. She lived there with her apprentices.

On arrival, mother and son noticed that it was dark except for the glow from a lone kerosene lantern in the hall. Their conversation alerted Robyn who was alone in the hall, she came to the door, unlocked it with the key and let them in. Mrs Wuta entered first, then Eric was sighted by Robyn. There was a hushed welcome.

"Hi Eric!"

and Eric responded with an equally hushed tone,

"Hi! Robyn!"

Mrs Wuta observed the couple carefully and sighed and said, "You youngsters are crafty. You have managed to hide your relationship all these several months. But the secret is now out. Let us sit down and take advantage of the time and have a little private talk."

Mrs Wuta broke the ice by addressing Robyn thus.

"Robyn, your uncle summoned Eric and me to an urgent meeting because of your condition. We had a brief meeting with him who in the absence of your late father has assumed the position of your substantive father according to our custom and also by law as per your late father's will. I am happy to inform you that he has taken on the assignment so seriously that he dared to label me as a mere Wuta and a stranger; but I quickly reminded him I am no less a Quinton-Taki than him and he agreed. In his capacity as family head, he ordered me to have a conversation with both of you to ascertain what are your thoughts so that we can forge a way forward. I must first inform you that Eric has confirmed that he is the father of the baby you are carrying in your womb and has made additional confessions which will sound better coming from his own mouth."

"Mother as I told you and uncle a little while ago, I love Robyn and I was happy to hear from you that she has also confirmed that she loves me."

"Robyn what do you say? Do you still love my son Eric?"

"Yes auntie, I do."

"Your uncle although very disappointed in the whole state of affairs, agrees that Eric being *yoobi* and you Robyn being *nunbi* can marry according to Ga custom, but he was surprised because when he mooted the idea albeit for family reasons, Eric invoked the rule of consanguinity and the importance of avoiding the practice of same. Paradoxically at the time he quoted that scientific principle he had already acted against it perhaps hoping that there would be no pregnancy. Now that a baby is on the way, we have serious problems to solve."

Eric was next to speak.

"Mother kindly explain the problems."

"The first problem has been solved by you Eric accepting responsibility for the pregnancy: all that follows is automatic.

Eric has to present drinks to Robyn's father in the person of his own uncle James to authenticate his acceptance of paternity of Robyn's expected baby. Eric will purchase the drinks tomorrow and I will present them. I should be accompanied by relatives from Eric's father's side but I will use my status as the widow to represent my late husband and present the drinks alone. We do not want too much gossip at the moment. Eric by presenting the paternity drinks, it would be presumed that you have agreed to look after the pregnant woman and the unborn child comprehensively meaning to provide her with adequate housing, clothing, feeding, hospital and antenatal, para-natal and post-natal care in addition to all other legitimate needs except sexual ones to which you are currently not entitled for reasons which will become clear sooner than later. You have no option but as a responsible man to accept all above; if for any reason you fail, your relatives who presented the drinks on your behalf would be held responsible, and you know what that means. Robyn is four months pregnant and fortunately she is healthy and strong, and there is no reason why we should not expect a normal delivery in five months. When the baby is born you will with our help organize the 'outdooring' and naming ceremony for the child according to Ga custom. You will give the child the appropriate Wuta family names. The surname will be Wuta of course but I will consult the living relatives of your father who are obliged to cooperate and suggest additional family identity names depending on the gender of the baby. The third and final problem will come after the naming of the child. It is complex and dependent on your emotions. You will have to decide honestly and from deep down your hearts whether to remain just parents of the child or get married which you are not obliged to. Impregnating a woman is not synonymous with marriage. You have five months to ponder over whether you would like to go your separate ways or remain together in wedlock. Your uncle the lawyer wants you to be patient and honest and wait for five long months before you make a pronouncement for obvious reasons."

Mrs Wuta then left the lovers on their own after warning them that she was not going to be far away for long, indeed she was only going to the kitchen to make three cups of cocoa drinks as a night cap after which Eric must be on his way to his uncle's mansion where he would spend the night alone. She then promised to join him and his uncle to present to him the drinks of acceptance of paternity of the unborn child and to bid him goodbye. Under the circumstances it was important for Eric to be seen rushing to his wife and son lest his relatives would be accused at a future date of promoting his relationship with Robyn – a relationship which had not been formalised traditionally.

Early the following morning Mrs Wuta bought the drinks as soon as the shops opened and rushed to her brother's mansion to meet him and Eric. It was a Saturday morning after breakfast. She met them on the veranda. After formal greetings, she made sure there were no eavesdroppers and then announced the purpose of her call. She cut the long story short as they were all aware of the real purpose of her call, she duly performed the ceremony and presented the drinks which were graciously accepted by the head of family Mr James Quinton-Taki. Papa James then addressed his nephew emphasising the significance of the ceremony. He commended and congratulated Eric on his maturity and the graciousness with which he had embraced his responsibilities as a man. Eric thanked them, bid his goodbye and rushed to Accra port to catch a boat to Sekondi.

While on the boat to Sekondi, Eric enjoyed several hours of solitude which enabled him to meditate in depth on current and future events. He arrived at several conclusions which he summarised as follows.

He would remain silent and not divulge anything concerning his amorous affairs with Robyn to his wife until the baby was born.

If any nosey person spilled the beans before the baby was born, he would deal with it to the best of his ability, in other words he would cross the river on sight.

Regular and frequent communication with his mother to whom he should send money for the upkeep of Robyn as he had solemnly pledged.

He would try to be a good husband to his wife and a good father to his sons.

When the baby was born in five months, he would declare his intentions to his wife specifically that he had acquired a second wife who had produced a baby. As for the unavoidable consequences which would certainly ensue, he was not prepared to speculate on at the moment.

He arrived at his home in Sekondi in the late afternoon and immediately put his plans into action. Fortunately, there was no hitch since nobody had spilt the beans. Obviously, his uncle and mother had kept the scandalous news hush hush, and the grapevine to Sekondi had been successfully kept in the dark so far, but he knew that all hell would break loose when the baby arrived and that was exactly what happened.

Five months went by like a flash. In the sixth month he knew that news would be coming through from Accra, and he regretted that he had not advised his mother to use a private courier as his uncle did when he communicated the news of Robyn's pregnancy. He knew that if the news arrived by ordinary morse code telegram it would spread like wildfire knowing the gossiping habit of the officers in the telegraph office. His worst fears materialised when that very afternoon he received a telegram from his mother which read 'A baby girl has been born.' Although the message was crisp and vague, to the experienced telegraph officer it was explicit. A gentleman who receives such a telegram must needs be connected intimately to the woman – most likely the father, grandfather, or uncle of the new baby. There are other possibilities, but they are all remote. As soon as Eric read the telegram, he knew he had to rush home to inform his wife before gossipers from the telegraph office did same.

Eric rushed home and at the front door he shouted, "Darling, I am home."

His wife shouted back from the lounge.

"You are home early, what's up?"

"Yes, I am early because I have something important to tell you. I hope the maids are far away. How is baby boy? Please sit down and listen carefully."

"I am all ears," she said while making herself comfortable in her favourite chair. "Baby has just fed and is fast asleep, maids have retired for their late afternoon rest in their quarters."

Eric then blurted out the naked truth saying, "I have acquired a new wife who has just delivered a baby girl. I received the telegram this afternoon."

Mrs Wuta, obviously shocked to the bones, managed to voice out the following: "A new wife in this town and I have not heard of it! That is impossible because I know all your movements, I am in touch with clever informers."

"I know you are, that is why I am very careful and absolutely clean in this wicked town. You should have asked me where the telegram came from. It was sent from my mother in Accra, she is currently looking after the woman and the baby."

"So your people knew all the time and they did not bother to tell my people as custom demands. Why?"

There was a long pause accompanied by weeping. She eventually recovered her composure and continued. "Eric Junior is barely three months old which means that you have been leading a double life. While pretending you were happy with the birth of your son you were making a new marriage on our blind side. Eric that was wicked and inhuman. Custom demands that you should obtain the consent of the first wife before taking a second wife, since you did not it is null and void and of no effect. I have nothing more to tell you. I will inform my relatives and they will help me to map my way forward."

Eric, sensing danger, initiated the reparation process at once by saying, "Please do not rush to any conclusions. A baby has been born, and the truth is that I am the father of that baby. I am aware that impregnating a woman is not tantamount to marriage. I have jumped the gun in two places by promising marriage to the young woman and by telling you moments ago that I have taken a second wife. I am very sorry; I should not have promised her people that I will marry her."

"Eric why did you rush to promise marriage? Is it because you were in a hurry to get rid of me? Now that I am still young, attractive and capable of having children I will leave you and go and find a new husband. You are welcome to this new wife, whoever she may be. I do not envy her; because if you are capable of doing this to me, she must be forewarned that you would eventually ditch her in the same manner. If ever I met the woman, I would advise her to be more vigilant than I have been because her new husband Eric would betray her one day.

Eric, I need to inform my people about these events. Who is this lady and where and when did you meet her?"

Eric knew instinctively that it would be better for Elsie his wife to learn all the facts from the horse's own mouth than from others, so he therefore decided to answer all her questions there and then.

"Her name is Robyn, and she is the daughter of my recently deceased uncle, that makes her my first cousin."

"How old is she and has she been to school?"

"She is seventeen years old and her schooling is nothing to write home about; not like you."

"Eric, you have callously done what is a taboo in most civilized societies by impregnating a teenaged illiterate cousin brought up on a farm in a village and decided to marry her in addition to your lawfully wedded wife who is currently nursing baby. How low can you sink? Tell me, are you marrying her for her inheritance or because you love her?"

These questions coming from his wife reminded him how intelligent and replete with female instinct his wife was. He recalled that his uncle James had suggested that he married Robyn in order to keep late farmer Jeff's wealth in the family. The irony then was that at the time when Eric protested against the suggestion on both moral and scientific grounds, he had already hypocritically and secretly had carnal knowledge of and impregnated his first cousin Robyn. James was naturally shocked when Eric accepted responsibility for the pregnancy and furthermore and declared eternal love for Robyn as it were confirming the well-known adage that, 'all is fair in love and war.' Eric was quick to realise that it would be imprudent to divulge any of the above facts so he decided to remain silent and let her draw whatever conclusions she preferred. Mrs Elsa Wuta, utterly shocked by the current state of affairs withdrew into her shelf and decided to do some hard thinking. Several liberal and compromising options came up in her mind but she rejected them all. She rather decided to quit in order to start a new life than to continue living with this irresponsible and thoroughly unpredictable man. She there and then made her thoughts known to Eric in no uncertain terms. The sooner she left the better, in any case it was imperative that she visited her people in Cape Coast without delay. Eric pleaded for time, he begged her to be patient and allow time to reveal other alternatives. The more he pleaded, the more he appeared like a hypocrite in her thoughts and the more resolute she became. She wasted no time, she put the sleeping baby on her back, made sure he was securely bound to her mid trunk with a strong cover cloth before she left the house. Her first place of call was the telegraph office where she composed a telegram to her mother:

I am coming home to-morrow STOP A domestic crisis has cropped up STOP Eric does not love me STOP

After dispatching the telegram, she returned to the house to pack her things and left for Cape Coast with the baby.

The sudden departure left a vacuum in the Wuta household and for the first time Eric realised that he had taken her for granted and that all along she had been the home maker and he had just tagged along. The void depressed him immensely. He was totally helpless. The house lost its lustre, things were difficult to find because of the general disorderliness and ordinary household hygiene became a problem. News of the recent events and the hurried departure of Mrs Wuta spread quickly along the gossiping grapevine of Sekondi and people started calling into the house to express their sympathies. The elderly men and his friends tried to cheer him up by inviting him to their homes for conversation, drinks and meals. The elderly women and wives of his friends were frantic about practical arrangements for regular meals and housekeeping. Despite the depth of the sympathies and all the help, the emptiness he felt within escalated by leaps and bounds to such a pitch that he had to do something sensible very fast or risk a mental breakdown. He sent two telegrams to Accra. The first to his mother and the second to his uncle. The wordings of the two were almost identical. The one to his mother was more desperate than the one to his uncle which was a business-like request for legal advice. His mother replied first saying that she would travel to Sekondi in three days to help him sort things out. Eric replied that she must postpone her plans because he felt that the first reparation attempt must be seen to have been initiated and executed by himself otherwise, he would be labelled a weakling and a mother's soft baby if she came to initiate the reparation process. Mother understood and postponed her coming. His uncle just gave a very short legal and practical advice that Eric must act like a man and must boldly but politely go and fetch his wife back. Even before lawyer James replied, Eric on deep reflection had decided to go to Cape Coast without delay to try and bring his wife back. He thanked his uncle for his wise counsel and added that he was already on his way to Cape Coast.

Eric regretted that he had allowed four whole days to pass by without making a move. He realised instead of allowing depression and lethargy to take hold of him he should have followed his wife to Cape Coast on the day she left. It was better late than never, and he further planned his strategy during the short trip. A lot of friends had offered to travel with him to give moral support, but he had arrived at a firm decision that his first attempt at reconciliation must be on his own, he therefore travelled to Cape Coast alone.

The meeting at Cape Coast was a disaster and it was all his fault. He had not fully realised the gravity of the situation, and he had been selfish to a fault by ignoring devastating effects of his actions on his wife.

On arrival at Mrs Wuta's family home in Cape Coast Eric was met by elders of the family including his mother-in-law. Elsa his wife however refused to come out of her room to meet him. The meeting therefore took place without her. The relatives were however very reasonable and polite to him because their aim was to preserve the marriage which was contracted not so long ago with so much promise. When Eric narrated his side of the story, which was full of mental flaws and misdemeanours they went to great lengths to point them out to him. They stressed that all marriages faced difficult moments and all married women could be emotional, temperamental and even impulsive at times, but eventually could be pacified if husbands showed remorse and maturity. They then pointed out to him that he jumped the gun when he reported to his wife that he had acquired a new wife, when by all standard practices he had not. He should endeavour to do all things correctly and as custom demanded. He should not have told his wife that he had married a second wife or even promised to marry his own cousin. He betrayed a propensity for immorality dreaded by all wives. He should have stuck to the naked truth well knowing that impregnating a concubine while legally married is common in our country and there are conventional ways of handling the misdemeanour. The standard procedure was that in order to avoid shot gun marriages which are frowned upon anyway, the naughty man's first duty was to accept responsibility for the mishap and name the child when it was born. The child must have a father at all costs. The question of marriage was irrelevant, and it was important to emphasise that Eric's insistence that he had already promised marriage to the pregnant woman was unacceptable; the so-called promise suggested that Eric neither loved nor respected her, furthermore that he did not value his legitimate marriage and the sons he had been blessed with. The right procedure would have been to organise the out-dooring of the new-born baby, give the child a name and then go separate ways so that the marriage remained intact.

Eric's mother-in-law insisted that it was the only way to save his marriage. At that point Mrs Wuta was persuaded to join the forum and Eric was requested to address the gathering which he did as follows:

"Mother-in-law and elders, there has been a little misunderstanding between my wife and me resulting in her leaving our marital home unceremoniously to come here. I am very sorry for the events that preceded her departure and I sincerely apologise for the distress you have all suffered. I beg all of you to allow me to take my wife back to Sekondi to enable us to sort things out amicably."

The elder brother of Eric's mother-in-law kept his cool and replied, "Eric, please do not ignore all that we told you prior to your wife joining us at this meeting. If you follow the guidelines we have outlined, I am sure you will be successful in your mission."

Eric remained stubborn and silent and Mrs Wuta burst out crying. His mother-in-law then spoke to Eric.

"Try not to upset your wife unduly, in any case you need counselling from your relatives. It is obvious that without your co-operation we cannot help you win back your wife who is an adult and we on our part will endorse whatever she decides to do. We advise you to go to your relatives to seek good advice and come back to meet us again."

Eric remained silent and stubborn, so the meeting came to an abrupt end and they all left the room leaving him alone to brood over his follies.

Eric's elderly uncle-in-law eventually returned to advise Eric to go and seek clarification of the customs from his elderly relatives. At that point Eric spoke thus: "I need to speak to my wife alone."

His uncle-in-law responded favourably by speaking aloud to the hearing of all: "Elsa your husband wishes to speak to you alone."

Mrs Wuta obliged and joined her husband. They spoke for ten minutes; when Eric realised that he could not persuade his tearful wife to accompany him to Sekondi, he left the premises without saying goodbye to his wife's relatives.

Eric spent the rest of the day in Cape Coast and left by the early morning boat to Sekondi. When the boat docked in the early afternoon, he rushed home. The emptiness and loneliness of his home without his family hit him hard and he faced the reality of losing valuable assets through sheer foolishness and stubbornness for the first time in his life. He slumped into his sofa and wept like a baby. He pulled himself together eventually, but he remained depressed and unable to do much. Meanwhile his absence had been noticed in the office, at the docks and also at the club. It was 6.00 pm and darkness was fast approaching when he heard a knock on the front door. On opening the door, he was confronted by his chief clerk and a small delegation from his office and two friends from the club whom he welcomed warmly. He tried to remain calm but they noticed his red eyes and dejectedness. They told him why they were there, and he thanked them for their kindness and concerns. He admitted he needed the company because he was not used to such loneliness. The club members then said they had come to take him to the club for some refreshment. He washed his face, combed his hair, changed his shirt and accompanied them to the club. At the club, kindness a friendliness exuded from all and sundry towards Eric such t recovery from depression albeit temporary, was clearly visib His spirits were uplifted, his appetite for conversation, beer a most importantly for food came back. He chatted away like times, drank a couple of bottles of beer with relish and ate the food presented to him and asked for more. The president the club rang his bell which traditionally called the members order paving the way to a short speech as follows.

"This club amongst other things is a welfare club, and as su we recognise each other's problems in order to face th collectively. Our brother Eric has presented us with a proble and we must help him. The first intervention is what has tak place to-night, but it is not enough. We must ask him about his immediate and long-term plans and effectively help him along. So, Eric what are your immediate plans?"

"My plan is to go to Accra to seek counselling from my uncle the lawyer, my mother and the entire extended family."

The president beamed with a spontaneous benevolent smile and said, "We commend you on your humility and assure you that you have taken the correct decision. You have stepped down from the stubbornness you displayed in Cape Coast which indeed was partly our fault in that we should not have allowed you to go to Cape Coast alone to face your wife and her relatives. This time around I insist that you must be accompanied, and I hereby propose that your chief clerk and one preferably two volunteers (including myself) accompany you on your impending voyage to Accra. First of all, for your personal safety because you are obviously depressed and

Cheering up Eric at Coast Club

secondly for counselling to ensure that you remain calm during the difficult discussions ahead."

Eric then responded to the president's kind remarks thus: "I will appreciate the companionship because the way I felt on my own at Cape Coast must not be repeated."

Plans were put in place for the journey to Accra and the evening's proceedings were brought to a successful end.

The president of the Sekondi club, an elderly and incredibly wise man had observed that Eric was by then dangerously depressed. He persuaded Eric's chief clerk and another young man from Wuta Maritime Enterprise to stay with Eric and look after him through the long night ahead of them. The next morning Eric's depression had indeed worsened and the president realised that the decision to avoid Eric being left entirely on his own was right. The boat to Accra was scheduled to depart at 6.00 am. When it did, there were on board Eric, the chief clerk and a junior clerk from Wuta Maritime, the president of Sekondi Club and another senior member from the club. They kept a close eye on Eric and his moods throughout the short voyage. They tried to cheer him up at every opportunity by tactfully maintaining a joyous holiday atmosphere throughout the short voyage. Eric had lost his appetite, but the happy atmosphere enabled him to drink something and eat during the journey. They arrived at Accra port at 6.00 pm and immediately set out by carriage to the Q-T mansions at Tudu. They were expected since the morse code telegram they sent in the morning before leaving Sekondi had arrived in Accra several hours before they did. They were welcomed according to custom by Mr and Mrs James Quinton-Taki Eric's uncle and his wife and a few other elderly relatives of the family including Mrs Catherine Wuta and two of her sisters and a brother. It was quite a sizeable gathering of about twenty including the delegation from Sekondi which numbered five made up of the Mr Cudjoe, president of the Sekondi club and his secretary, the chief clerk of Wuta Maritime Company and his two assistants. After the initial salutations and offering of drinking water to the visitors, the host's linguist asked them to state the purpose of their visitation. As Eric was too depressed to speak, by mutual consent the president of Sekondi club had been selected as spokesman. Mr Cudjoe went straight to the heart of the matter and spoke thus.

"Elders here assembled, I greet you well. I thank you for your kindness in receiving our delegation so cordially and at such a short notice. We are here on behalf of our very good friend Eric who is your relative. The details of the problem at hand are well known to you and we are sure you have a far better understanding of the complexity than we have. We have already had a prolonged conversation with our friend and told him that he jumped the gun when he told his wife and relatives that he had acquired a new wife or more specifically that he had promised marriage to a young woman he had impregnated. We have told him that we endorse the advice given to him by his wife's relatives that he must seek counselling from you in order to change his current mindset to a more conventional mode to facilitate reconciliation with his wife. We are here to help him to seek wise counselling from you so that he rejects what is wrong and does what is right."

The head of family lawyer James Q-T responded.

"On my own behalf and on behalf of this family I now welcome and thank you formally and state categorically that you have done very well to accompany, sustain and support our son. I know my nephew well, and I can confidently state that he is my friend, being his uncle and several years older than him notwithstanding. Under ordinary circumstances he is very cheerful and full of life. Right now, he is a shadow of himself; in short, he is depressed because the correct line of action has been delayed and my sister Catherine and my very self are partially to blame. When the problem first came to our attention, Eric insisted that as an adult, he wished to proceed without his mother's interference and we gave in, but not before we had explained the custom to him. We totally agree with you that he jumped the gun when he promised marriage to my niece Robyn following the birth of the baby."

Addressing Eric directly he continued, "Eric, we love you and we will help you to do the right thing which is to get your wife back with you at Sekondi. Your mother has already complied with your instructions and presented the acceptance drink, signifying that you impregnated Robyn and that you are the biological and spiritual father of the newly born baby girl. The baby will be out-doored according to Ga custom, and given a name by you aided by your late father's family. The mother of the baby girl has been counselled by her aunts and has accepted the traditional rules of our society. According to those rules the two of you are not obliged to marry, but rather go your separate ways now and allow nature to take care of the future. Our pressing duty now is to preserve your current marriage by facilitating reconciliation. The immediate plan is to rush to Cape Coast to plead with your wife and her relatives to forgive and forget your waywardness. We will inform them immediately that they should expect us the day after to-morrow. I will lead the delegation myself. Unless anybody has something very important to say I declare by the powers invested in me as head of this family that this meeting is closed. The night is not so young at the moment and tomorrow is a working day for some of us. You who have come on a long voyage will need to rest in order to be fit for the task which awaits us in Cape Coast the day after tomorrow. Dinner has been served, and I hereby invite all of you to take a drink and dine with us."

They all trooped to the veranda on the other side of the Q-T mansion where preparations had been made during the meeting. It was a buffet dinner. Assorted drinks were served: liberal potions of beer, lemonade, whisky and wines were there for the choosing. It was a lively festive occasion and the visitors from Sekondi marvelled at the high level of sophistication in the Q-T household. They helped themselves to heaps of the choicest dishes and it was truly a joyous occasion.

Eric drifted to his mother's side and asked for her attention for a few minutes. "Mother, are you aware that I have not seen the baby? Can I see her at all, or will I be breaking some rule if I do?"

His mother replied without hesitation. "Of course, you can see the little girl, after all she is your own daughter, you can even see her mother too, but I will be in the room to act as chaperon when you see Robyn for obvious reasons. We intentionally left tomorrow free so that those exigencies could be taken care of."

Eric was thoroughly satisfied by his mother's answers and indeed the weight of depression mingled with anxiety suddenly left him and he almost felt like his old self again. He re-joined the crowd and thenceforth fully participated in the convivialities with his friends who noticed the change in him for the better and were very pleased.

The evening activities ended around 9.30 pm and they all retired to bedrooms prepared for them in this very large Q-T mansion. Eric armed with the knowledge that he was going to see Robyn and her baby in the morning felt at peace and slept very well. He was woken up by a knock on his door at 6.30 am and told that the bathroom was ready for him. He went downstairs, took a warm bath and came back to his room and dressed up. At 8.00 am he was in the dining room to meet the rest of the visitors. They were very happy to see him in a cheerful mood, and he told them the secret which had given him a good night's rest and virtually snapped him from the dangerous depression he had suffered over the past week. After breakfast a city tour was arranged for the visitors from Sekondi except Eric. They were packed into a carriage and driven to town to visit the tourist sites which included the Christiansborg Castle and its beautiful gardens, the magnificent Town Hall, the Ga Mantse's Palace, the Accra Lighthouse and the fishermen's landing beaches. Eric on the other hand was instructed to wait on the veranda for a young relative who had been asked by Eric's mother to accompany him to her home. The young man arrived 30 minutes after the tourists had left, and he and Eric took a long walk to Mrs Wuta's humble home in central Accra. That really was the family home and the original abode of the Stonewall Quinton-Taki, the father of late Jeff the farmer, James the lawyer and Catherine, Eric's mother.

As soon as Eric arrived, he was ushered into a room where mother and baby girl were waiting for him. Eric smiled a good morning to Robyn the new mother who responded graciously with a broad smile. Eric then approached mother and baby, congratulated Robyn with an innocent handshake and proceeded to take a close look at the baby in the lap of her mother Robyn. Mrs Wuta broke the ice by speaking to the new-born baby.

"Martha your daddy is here to see you," and as if by magic baby opened her eyes, looked at Eric and gave a broad baby grin. Eric was moved to a combination of joy and sorrow. He gathered the baby into his arms and said,

"Hello!" while the two women mother and grandmother looked on in amazement. Eric then remarked, "What a beautiful baby! Whom does she resemble?"

Mrs Wuta was quick to answer.

"She resembles both of you for obvious reasons, the best one being that baby's parents resemble each other."

Mrs Wuta remarked further,

"All her structures are perfect, she is going to be tall and shapely, and as a young woman she will be the toast of the whole town."

Eric then said, "I agree with you mother, she is truly beautiful, look at those straight long shapely legs and perfectly moulded feet and pretty tiny toes. I can even now imagine how she will look like as a young woman. Robyn thank you for giving us such a beautiful baby."

Robyn spoke at length for the first time.

"Thank you too, after all said and done although I alone carried her for 9 months, in reality she is half yours. I thought she resembled only you but now that Aunt Kate has alerted me to other details, I will watch baby closely looking out for wherein she resembles you or me."

Mrs Wuta characteristically quickly remarked. "You will not be able to tell because she resembles both of you who in turn resemble each other. Eric, take baby to the veranda for fresh air and hug her for a long while to develop a bond, and remember to promise her that as long as you are alive, she will lack nothing."

"Mother I most certainly promise just that wholeheartedly."

CHAPTER FOUR

MARRIAGE-SALVAGING EXPEDITION TO CAPE COAST

The following day was a Thursday. Apart from the activities already described, the day was also used to send telegrams to Cape Coast to inform Eric's wife that a high-powered delegation from her husband's family including the head of family Lawyer James Quinton-Taki would be arriving the following day and would be grateful for an audience for the purpose of preserving the marriage. Friday was earmarked for the journey which was scheduled to start early with the first passenger boat. Departure from Accra was to be at 6.00 am and arrival at Cape Coast, barring any mishaps and by the grace of God, was to be at 2.30 pm; just in time for the meeting at 3.00 pm.

When they arrived at Mrs Elsie Wuta's family home, they were ushered into a large sitting room where they found seated at the far end elders of the family all very well dressed and looking dignified. The visitors greeted all the seated elders in the front row, mostly men with hearty handshakes, then raised their hands and saluted the other men and the elderly women of the family in the back rows with a bow and broad smiles. They were then directed into their seats to face their hosts. Lawyer James Q-T sat at the centre in the front row, flanking him to his right and left were his male relatives from Accra, and Eric's friends from Sekondi respectively; Eric's mother and Eric himself sat to the immediate left and right of Q-T. The scene was thus perfectly set for the serious and formal discussions. The head of the household started the meeting. He thanked the visitors for their wise and timely visit, introduced the family members with him and then asked the household servants to give them water to drink. He then stated that they received the telegram alerting them of the impending visitation in good time and as was evident from the current set up, they hurriedly embarked

Marriage-salvaging meeting at Cape Coast

on preparations all morning to assemble the important people the distinguished visitors had requested or needed to meet.

He then formally enquired thus: “What important or urgent business has dragged you from your comfortable homes and busy schedules and motivated you to endure a hazardous journey to visit our humble home?”

It was then the turn of the leader of the visiting delegation to respond to the magnificent display of indigenous linguistics. James Q-T appropriately rose up to the occasion and said,

“I thank you all here assembled for welcoming us so warmly. Your kindness and hospitality, already well known to some of us, has been surpassed today by this display of noble civility of responding so graciously to our desperate call at such a short notice. You rightly asked what our urgent business is, and we hereby state humbly and unequivocally that we are here to try to salvage the hitherto good marriage of our son Eric and your beautiful daughter Elsie. We have already admonished our son that he should not have allowed his youthful exuberance and excessive libido to drive him out of control to yield to the temptations of the flesh. The wrong he has committed is so enormous that in the eyes of the almighty God it is a sin. It is with a sense of shame that I am obliged to inform you that the girl Eric has had a baby with is my late brother’s daughter and indeed my daughter, now that the family in its wisdom gave her to me following the death of her father. In other words, Eric, your son-in-law has had carnal knowledge of his biological first cousin, or to put it more bluntly under our Ga custom his own sister. We are all aware that Eric and his sister have had an incestuous affair which is considered a taboo amongst our people, and furthermore frowned upon in the scientific world because when babies result from consanguineous marriages, they tend to bear serious disabilities. Such marriages must be avoided at all costs and the family I represent hereby rejects such a move. Even more importantly it is the family's entrenched opinion that Eric jumped the gun when he proposed marriage to the young girl when he discovered that he had impregnated her because according to well established Ga custom impregnation is not synonymous to marriage. Eric is already married according to Ga custom and also by the ordinance in the Methodist Church. I am a lawyer and I have carefully explained to Eric that bigamy is a criminal offence in this country known as the Gold Coast whose laws are 100% British. Bigamy is a serious criminal offence punishable by a long period of imprisonment without the option of a fine. Who in this room wants Eric to go to prison for several years?

"I pause for an answer.

"Since nobody wants Eric to go to prison, let us just settle for what our elders have prescribed as acceptable remedy for such situations. It is important to appreciate that the young girl whom Eric Wuta had rudely violated and impregnated and finally produced a daughter with is my niece and legitimate ward. Her extended family, whose head is my very self, have already communicated the customarily requirements to him. Marriage is out of the question and he knows it just as well as the girl with whom he had the baby. Eric has already provided the customarily drinks to accept that he fathered Robyn's baby, which implies that he will be entirely responsible for all the needs of the baby until she becomes an adult and capable of looking after herself. Now that the baby has been born, Eric and Robyn have no responsibilities towards each other; indeed they will be actively persuaded or forced, if necessary, to go their separate ways. It is over between them and I have by the powers invested in me as head of family ordered them to drift far apart and 'sin no more.'"

The head of family responded to the learned pleadings in equally eloquent and erudite terms as follows.

"On my own behalf and on behalf of my relatives gathered here I thank you most sincerely for addressing us this blessed afternoon. You have spoken well and wisely. We have perfectly understood your message and in order to produce a truthful unambiguous response you must bear with us for a few minutes while we retire for consultations: meanwhile we will demonstrate our goodwill and hospitality by providing you with refreshment; please be patient."

Mrs Elsa Wuta and her family members ably led by their family head who incidentally was also the maternal uncle of Elsa duly retired into chambers for urgent consultations. Meanwhile the visiting delegation was served with a variety of soft drinks and tray loads of delicious home-made typical Fante small chops. The visitors, half-starving in the late afternoon dug into the refreshment with relish while they engaged in hearty small talk well knowing from the way the reception had proceeded so far that they were heading towards a successful salvage of the marriage. They did not have to wait a long time for the anticipated good news. The host delegation was back in their seats ready for the meeting to resume in exactly 30 minutes.

The meeting was called to order as soon as Elsa's uncle Opanyin Gyebi, was seated. He immediately started addressing the gathering in his usual dignified manner.

"Ladies and gentlemen, I bring you good news!"

That very short statement engendered a prolonged loud applause. Opanyin had to resort to all his skills of presiding over family meetings to bring the gathering to order in order to continue his address.

"I am happy to inform you that the consultations have proved fruitful. Firstly, Elsa's family elders agreed that, despite the naughty youthful waywardness of their daughter's husband, their beautiful marriage which had already been blessed with two healthy sons must be encouraged to continue so that God willing their precious daughter may produce more children for the family, bearing in mind that in the Akan tradition all children ensuing from a marriage belong to the maternal family, in other words to us sitting on this side of the gathering. Regarding our aggrieved daughter Elsa, I must confess that it proved to be the most difficult part of the negotiation. She had lost trust in her husband because to put it in her own words; 'she was completely unaware of the affair and she was hit by a bomb from her blind side and even as we were talking to her, she was still very dizzy and trying hard to recover.' Mrs Elsa Wuta no doubt to all those who know her well is a very well brought up God-fearing woman. After gentle persuasion by her own family members whom she adored, she agreed to yield to our request on one very important condition. The condition was that we should call Eric to the family caucus meeting remote from his family members, observe his demeanour, scrutinize his answers to difficult searching questions and determine in all honesty whether there was enough remorse, respect and love in him after such dastardly behaviour to facilitate reconciliation and restoration of the marriage between us."

The experienced lawyer James Quintin-Taki was quick to recognize the value of the pending interrogation and therefore granted the seemingly odd request without hesitation while others, less experienced, protested in vain. Eric willingly went to the hearing in camera and obviously passed the difficult test with flying colours testified by his return smiling to his relatives in less than ten minutes.

The plenary session resumed as soon as the host delegation took their seats facing the visitors. Elsa's uncle apologised for keeping them waiting, thanked them profusely for their patience and sincerely hoped that they were well looked after and refreshed during the rather prolonged interlude. He then addressed them formally as follows:

"Distinguished ladies and gentlemen and beloved in-laws here assembled, I bring you good news; we first of all listened to the point of view of our daughter who insisted that we must observe the attitude and listen to her husband before we ventured to advise the reconciliation we so earnestly desired. We complied and interviewed Eric your son whom I am pleased to inform you performed to our satisfaction. Reconciliation sealed with a dutiful and 'passionate' embrace took place, and I hereby order them to repeat same now and in the presence of all of us here gathered."

The couple Mr and Mrs Wuta stood up and walked from their places and stood between the two family groups and heartily embraced to spontaneous thunderous applause. At that very moment all became aware that reconciliation had occurred. Lawyer James Quiton-Taki the leader of the visiting delegation begged for attention to speak. After several efforts the noise level reduced to a reasonable level and he remarked:

"On my own behalf and on behalf of my nephew Eric and his dear wife Elsa and last but not the least the concerned family members and friends of Eric thank the Almighty God for giving us this glorious day and a modicum of his wisdom which has enabled us to act wisely proving beyond all reasonable doubt that we are created in his own image. Secondly, I thank the principal host and his good people here assembled for rendering our visit and deliberations useful and fruitful. We the visitors dare not take any more of their precious time, on that note all that remains is for us to get up from our comfortable seats, walk over to their seats and thank each and every one of them with a warm handshake and exit the premises fully satisfied and at peace."

Long before they dared leave their seats, Opanyin, the hosting family head announced very loudly thus:

"Attention please! The meeting has not been adjourned; the learned lawyer has jumped the gun. It was I your humble servant who declared the meeting opened earlier on in the afternoon, therefore it is my sole duty to close it formally; but before I do so I have an announcement which is as follows: Mrs Elsa Wuta and her family members of Cape Coast respectfully invite you all to dinner at these premises as soon as the meeting ends formally. May I now request the reverend minister to say the closing prayers."

After the brief closing prayers, the presiding host declared the meeting closed but warned that nobody was to leave and that the family would be pleased to enjoy dinner with all, that being the usual tradition in Cape Coast.

It was a buffet dinner preceded of course by cocktails of non-alcoholic as well as alcoholic ones such as beer wines and spirits except the locally distilled akpeteshie which was frowned upon at formal events. The dinner was very good, typically Cape Coast fresh sea food cuisine of a large variety of fish, shrimps, lobsters and crabs prepared in the inimitable Fantsi-Fantsi style plus an equally assorted cooked, baked, fried, steamed, roasted and mashed yam, sweet potatoes, cocoyam, kenkey, banku, plantain cakes and sweetened or spiced porridges of bambara beans and black-eyed beans. Dessert was of course strictly European and consisted of a variety of cakes, pancakes, sweet breads and custards. Informal small talk followed in small groups and new acquaintances were forged naturally. It was now early evening and time for the visiting delegation to depart, but before they did the leader of the delegation, Lawyer James Quintin-Taki sought permission to speak and was given clearance graciously by the chief host in the person of Panyin Atakora Gyebi.

"On behalf of the visiting delegation of relatives and friends and on my own behalf l thank the entire family of Mrs Elsa Wuta for the sumptuous dinner which I dare say was a pleasant and unexpected surprise because we came here this afternoon on a sensitive mission. The outcome of the meeting was very good and we are proud to repeat the gratitude we expressed earlier. The dinner was indeed a bonus we did not anticipate in our wildest dreams, but it happened and we sincerely thank you for it. Above all we thank God for the miraculous events he has bestowed on us. It is now time for us to leave. Eric has whispered into my ear that he is staying here rather than come with us to Accra; my answer is that it is good news and overwhelming evidence that our mission has been successful."

IMMEDIATE POST-VISITATION EVENTS

The two groups of visitors from Accra and Sekondi respectively left the dinner at Elsa's family home in Cape Coast in a very happy mood, fully satisfied that they had done a good job. The group from Sekondi found a passenger boat due to depart later that same evening for the short voyage to Sekondi and they hurriedly embarked for the journey. The group from Accra was not so lucky in that the last boat to Accra had already sailed, therefore they settled for overnight stay at a comfortable inn not far from the Cape Coast port. The night was still young so they were invited by the leader of the delegation for drinks at the bar. It was a happy celebration for a truly successful exercise spiced by numerous hilarious anecdotes and jokes by all and sundry. Suddenly they realized that midnight was round the corner, and since they were booked to leave port on the 6.00 am boat, they needed to retire to bed to enjoy some rest and sleep in order to be up and ready for the boat trip to Accra.

The boat ride to Accra that Saturday morning was uneventful. No formal meetings were scheduled, leaving the delegates free to enjoy the ride with informal conversations and drinks on the breezy but sunny decks while the boat sailed smoothly eastwards to Accra. Uncle Kobby, the oldest relative on board requested a short private meeting with the leader of the delegation lawyer James Q-T. Kobby was by then the only surviving sibling of the late Stonewall Quintin-Taki, the late father of James Q-T. Despite his age was very agile and had a sharp intellect, and furthermore he was always willing to offer good suggestions on the most difficult subjects. He had been brought on this trip to do just that, and therefore his nephew James was eager to hear what he had to say especially since he had not spoken much during the whole episode.

The two elderly gentlemen men found two comfortable chairs at the far corner of the lounge conveniently remote and therefore out of ear-short for their private chat. The older gentleman who had requested the meeting started without delay by addressing his nephew in the manner they were both accustomed to.

"My learned nephew I requested this meeting and so it is my prerogative to begin, although the matter concerns me, I am also aware that it concerns you more directly being the legal guardian of the new mother who indeed is still a minor in the eyes of the law, so I beg you to be patient and forgive me in advance for being unduly presumptuous."

"Uncle Kobby you are forgiven, please go ahead and have your say."

"In the first-place things went too smoothly at the meeting with our in-laws. In other words, your nephew got away with his abominable behaviour too easily, and our in-laws perhaps urged on by Elsa were too kind to him and I suspect it is nothing but the proverbial calm before the storm. In the first place you and I belong to a family blessed with extremely good looks both the women and the men and there seems to exist a family curse which rears its head every now and then leading invariably to deep physical attraction ending with incest as we are confronted with currently. I am not quite sure you are old enough to remember that what we are currently battling with has happened before in living memory. I can clearly recall two previous episodes and my dear late mother recounted a third and warned me never to divulge same."

"Uncle, I am aware of more than one such case which I am not prepared to talk about because as the saying goes 'the walls have ears', nevertheless, go ahead and make your point about this particular case."

"The important point I wish to make is that it has all been too easy for Eric, therefore it can happen again. Secondly, I can easily foresee a repeat involving another couple in the near or distant future. We must plan carefully to prevent an immediate recurrence involving Eric and Robyn; your vague warning that they should drift far apart and 'go and sin no more' is too biblical and mere talk -- the average Gold Coast native does not fear the Bible."

"Uncle, you are indeed a wise man and the family is lucky to have you around. My statement at the meeting was a mere play on words to the gallery. I have plans which if and when properly executed would physically separate the naughty rascals for a long time, but we must be patient and endeavour to interview the young lady even more thoroughly than we have Eric. I will insist on you being present at that interview. I can assure you that besides my sister Kate no other person will be there, in other words it will be an entirely a Quintin-Taki inner caucus affair."

He paused for the old man's comments.

"So far so good; please carry on and tell me more, after all you are in charge and I am only an important advisor."

"My good sister Kate -- who is currently looking after the young mother and baby -- and I have been advised by our family doctor to tread gently and cautiously with our plans because under even better or normal circumstances young mothers can suffer from a condition known in medical circles as 'post-delivery melancholia' which can render a young mother extremely depressed to the extent of rejecting the baby or threatening suicide or both. It is important therefore to assess the situation and seek medical assistance if necessary before we proceed with our plans. As regards your fears for a repetition in the family, I feel same, bearing in mind that I also have young children of the same breed as Eric and Robyn and prevention of the 'family curse' will be up most in my mind henceforth."

"Son, I agree with all that you have said, and will co-operate to achieve the desired results, God willing."

They safely arrived at Accra port at dusk on at typical Saturday when the city was in its usual festive mood. The colonial authorities in their eagerness to extract maximum productivity from the natives had prescribed a 6-day working week in the Gold Coast as against 5 days in their own country. Saturday night was therefore special in that it was the only night not followed by a working day, thus enabling all workers young and old the freedom to enjoy full scale entertainment at private house parties, concerts, dances, ballroom and street revelries, and so on without the burden of having to get up early for work the following day. They enjoyed the loud music all the way to the Quintin-Taki mansion where a sumptuous dinner prepared by the lady of the house awaited them.

The meeting at Kate Wuta's modest house in the heart of bustling Accra township started at exactly 12.30 pm when lawyer James and his uncle Cobbinah joined the two women, namely the elderly Kate and Robyn with her new-born baby Martha in the bedroom assigned to Robyn. After the usual preliminary greetings and pleasantries mostly directed to the sleeping baby, they all settled in comfortable armchairs and the meeting started in earnest, but not before Kate was sure that all the maids and hangers-on had been ordered out of the main building. The head of family welcomed them formally and announced the business of the meeting which was to review what happened at the meeting in Cape Coast and to plan the way forward. He gave a short report of the consensus amicably achieved at Cape Coast for the benefit of Robyn who was of course absent at that meeting and he spoke directly to the young mother.

"My dear daughter Robyn, I can assure that it was a friendly meeting and the discussions were cordial and civilised. We disabused the rumour that a marriage had occurred between you Robyn and your cousin. We assured them that we had already explained the traditional rules that govern the delicate issue of a man impregnating a woman out of wedlock, to wit that mere impregnation and producing a baby do not constitute a marriage. Eric admitted that he had erred on both moral and legal grounds and he begged his wife and her relatives for forgiveness. They forgave him on strict conditions which they knew could not be met without the cooperation of you Robyn and us the family elders represented here by myself, your aunt Kate and your grand uncle. The gist of the condition is that you and Eric must not be allowed to meet anywhere. Eric will continue looking after the baby by providing funds channelled through us. Eric's responsibility to you ended when Martha was born, and you were discharged in good health by the medical team which supervised the ante natal and post-natal services. It is now my onerous duty to ask you my dear daughter whether you fully understand the conditions and can fully satisfy them."

Robyn kept her calm composure, took in a deep breath and answered the difficult question thus:

"Uncle I understand the question perfectly and I thank you for asking it. Before I answer the question kindly permit me to make a few remarks. First despite the wide age difference between Eric and me, the events which led to the pregnancy were not due his actions alone; in other words, there was mutual consent, in that sometimes I went to him willingly and other times he came to me willingly. Secondly, I always knew that he was legally married and what we were doing was wrong; we both sinned and I have regretted what I did, I know the wrong must not be repeated and I pray every day to God for forgiveness and I hope he is doing same. Your report implying that his wife and her people have forgiven him has lifted a heavy burden off my conscience. Finally, to answer your question, may I say in all honesty that I am willing to satisfy all the conditions you so eloquently stated in your opening statement."

Mrs Kate Wuta Eric's mother was the next to speak and she spoke almost in anger but with civility and utmost restraint.

"Robyn my daughter you have spoken well, and I am impressed with your maturity. However, I object to your near impudent attempt to suggest that Eric must not be held totally responsible for what happened. Your uncle is an eminent lawyer and if he is reluctant to tell you the truth, I am not so inclined. Eric is my son and I can state categorically without any fear of contradiction that by all standards he has taken advantage of your youth and naivety. In the eyes of the law of this colony you were a minor when he had carnal knowledge and indeed you are still a minor since you are still under 18 years old and should Eric be tried under British law by a white judge there is no doubt in my mind that he would be imprisoned despite your precocious protestations that the act took place with your consent. The law is grey and confused in this country because child marriage is practised in some native communities and they get away with them because they are not reported. Eric is my son and he has disappointed me for his lack of self-control leading to the serious sin of incest despite all the moral and religious training his late father and I imparted to him. But alas the harm has already been done and we are here on a salvaging or reparation mission and we must be constructive in our criticisms. I am therefore prepared to forgive but let me repeat that you have no right whatsoever to defend him legally or morally. However, as I said earlier, I admire your maturity and fortitude and your willingness without any prompting to fulfil all the conditions proposed in Cape Coast. With permission from your two uncles, I wish to ask how you plan to effect the physical separation and your uncle's admonition of 'go and sin no more.' I pause for an answer."

"Thank you, Auntie, for the opportunity to outline my future plans. Formal education from elementary all the way through secondary school right up to the tertiary level is my immediate plan. When my father was alive, he made the plans and indeed he actually put money aside monthly for the project. Unfortunately, his unexpected illness and death aborted the plan. The good news is that he told me the details of the plan and I intend implementing the same with your help and the help of God. I need to tell you the plan because I know you will all like it because it guarantees the physical separation which the meeting at Cape Coast so urgently and rightly so desires. My father had identified a famous school for adults like me or even older in Port Calabar in South eastern Nigeria where he had plans to send me."

"How did he plan to finance that novel and expensive foreign education?" asked Mrs Wuta.

To her utter surprise Robyn responded with utmost alacrity. "My father assured me that he was putting a stipulated sum of £2 into an envelope locked in his safe monthly for the purpose. On one occasion, about a year before he died, he actually showed me the heavily stuffed envelope. He said that for the plan to work the total amount required for the adult elementary school of four years duration and the concentrated and abridged secondary education of four years which would see me through matriculation and ready to enter a university or the Inns of court in London to do law should be deposited in a bank in London. He was in the process of arranging with my maternal aunt who lives in Calabar for the elementary and secondary parts of my education when he died. I would be very grateful if my living father lawyer James Quinton-Taki would kindly revive those plans and ensure both my education and the physical separation from cousin Eric."

"Before your uncle James speaks, I wish to know your plans for the baby."

Once again her well organised answer shocked her aunt.

Without hesitation Robyn said.

"Martha is my baby and I plan to take her with me."

While Mrs Wuta was recovering from the shock, lawyer James broke the ice.

"Robyn is quite right; the envelope and her father's plans for her education are safe and I promise here and now that I will revive the plans without delay."

Mrs Wuta, encouraged by her brother's generosity, assured Robyn and her two uncles that baby Martha was precious and loved by the whole family and as soon she was weaned from her mother's priceless breast milk, her mother could safely go and pursue her education abroad while the baby was taken care of by her grandparents in this very home.

"Well, Uncle, you will agree with me that we have had a good meeting such that all our problems have been solved happily by no less than five Quinton-Takis belonging to three generations. I am sure our late father is here with us not in the flesh but at least well represented by his beautiful picture on the wall in the hall. Good old Stonewall! your people are not doing badly at all. Today we have taken good decisions and what remains is to put our shoulders to the wheel and push hard along the steep slope of the problem and surely with the help of the almighty God in heaven success will crown our efforts. Two Quinton-Taki gentlemen now wish to take leave of the three Quinton-Taki ladies. When God-willing we meet again in a day or two I will report the progress we have made."

The two elderly gentlemen then departed the scene leaving their indefatigable sister alone to look after her niece and her baby.

James Q-T arrived at his mansion that Sunday afternoon at 2.00 pm and encountered his extremely upset wife because he was late for Sunday lunch which was by family convention scheduled for 1.30 pm sharp. The good lady was loitering on the porch when her husband arrived equally upset and obviously remorseful. Mrs Q-T who never failed to demand explanations for irregular actions regardless of the mood of her husband characteristically confronted her husband with a battery of questions. On this occasion James remained calm and stated that he attended the planned Quinton-Taki family meeting after church at his sister Kate's house which unexpectedly dragged on far longer than they had expected.

"I am very sorry to be late for lunch and since I am genuinely starving, please let us enjoy this belated lunch before I narrate to you the complex and rather interesting and satisfactory outcome of the meeting."

Mrs Q-T agreed and they had lunch without much conversation, a most unusual occurrence.

After the lunch, which was very good, Q-T strolled around the house for a few minutes to allow the food to settle properly in the stomach, he then hurried to the upstairs bedroom for his usual Sunday afternoon siesta. The dutiful and loving wife followed her husband upstairs without delay. She was determined to get some information before the old man dozed off because she knew from previous experience that if she allowed the old man to fall asleep it would take three or four hours of deep slumber for him to earn enough sleep and thus be fully awake and alert to produce a coherent story. Q-T was the first to speak.

"I know why you are here; you want me to say something before I doze off! Well, we had a very good meeting at my sister's house, Uncle Kobby was there, so were Robyn and her baby Martha. The long and short of it all was that Robyn, on request, laid bare her plans for her future, plans which will facilitate and ensure her physical separation from Eric and at the same time encourage her own development."

"I am all ears, please carry on."

"Robyn made it absolutely clear that her plan is to acquire formal education from primary school which she unfortunately missed in the village, followed by secondary school in order to achieve matriculation to enable her to acquire tertiary education with the law profession as the ultimate target. Her late father before he died had identified a famous rapid results school in Calabar City in faraway Southern Nigeria for her primary and secondary education. The tertiary level will be undertaken in England."

"I have two questions. How was her education abroad going to be funded and what does she want to do about the baby?"

"You women think alike. Kate asked the same questions and Robyn came up with readymade and well-rehearsed answers."

"Tell me the answers."

Before he spoke Q-T got out of the bed and moved to the other end of the room where his late brother's safe had been placed next to his own since it was brought from the village. He first of all opened his own safe, took out the keys of his brother's safe and opened same with ease. He pulled out a heavily stuffed brown envelope and returned to join his wife in bed.

"Robyn referred to this envelope to answer the first question you have just asked, which incidentally was the exact question put to her rather too aggressively by Kate. Robyn told us that on the several occasions when her father discussed the education plans, he showed her this envelope stuffed with money saved monthly over several years and earmarked for her education abroad. Unfortunately, he died before he could implement the plans which had been spelt out in detail. Well Robyn spoke the truth at the meeting. There is a lot of money stuffed in here, and the plans are also here. Please take a look at the contents of this document, while I attempt to check the money."

Q-T then noticed that the money was in several denominations including coins. He stopped and said, "I cannot do this. I should rather take it to the British Bank of West Africa on the High Street tomorrow and ask the young white manager to get the money sorted out and counted professionally and deposited in the family account: do you think that is a good idea?"

"It is a good idea and something which should have been done a long while ago. Remember you are supposed to hold all your brother's properties in trust until Robyn reaches the age of twenty one, when you will be obliged to hand over to her."

"I know, I kept procrastinating, in any case as the sages say it is better late than never."

"Now what about my second question?"

"Oh! That one. Robyn says the baby is hers and she will take Martha to Nigeria."

Mrs Q-T exclaimed: "No, no, no."

Her husband once again remarked that women indeed think alike and added, "Kate responded in exactly the same manner this afternoon and stated categorically that mother and baby in a strange land and with mother in school full time should not be condoned by the family. My sister further suggested that Robyn under those circumstances would have to engage strangers to look after Martha and that could be dangerous for both. We all agreed and, in the end, reached a consensus that if the preparations for Robyn's trip to Nigeria were started now, it would take some time to finalise same, bearing in mind the slow pace of communication between the Gold Coast and Nigeria. We further agreed that in about a year from now when the baby has been weaned will be the best time for Robyn to start her programme in Calabar, leaving baby Martha under the able and tender care of Grandmother Kate Wuta and the rest of the family. In the next few days, or better still tomorrow I will write a letter addressed to Robyn's maternal aunt named in the plan to ascertain her willingness and/or preparedness to accommodate Robyn and to start the enrolment process even now, so that God willing she should be able to start her adult schooling next year. Robyn is a bright girl and I am sure she will be able to matriculate in eight years or even seven years, four for primary and three for secondary or vice versa. The primary is usually more difficult for adults. It has been observed once the adult student masters the rules of numbers and fundamentals of arithmetic plus a good working knowledge of idiomatic English and is able to read and understand long texts, and also comprehend spoken English at normal speed, and put it all down on paper, the secondary education becomes a piece of cake. Robyn is already fairly literate in Ga. She has rudiments of the English language therefore I am quite sure she will do very well."

"James, by the way, is the money in the envelope enough to take care of tertiary education in England?"

"Do not worry, where there is the will, there is a way. There is plenty of money in that envelope, besides the farm at Pakro is still very productive and as you are aware Robyn owns that farm."

Q-T then jumped out of the bed and put the envelope back into the safe, locked both safes and hopped back into bed.

"Let us rest and sleep for a while for tomorrow will definitely be a very busy day for me."

The sympathetic wife agreed, and Q-T dozed off immediately into a deep slumber while Mrs Q-T remained wide awake daydreaming about her own children and wondering whether her selfless husband would not be distracted by the current Robyn affairs to the detriment of his own children. She swore that she would do everything possible to ensure that they would all acquire tertiary education in England. She realised that her late brother-in-law's strategy was good therefore in the morning she would discuss the possibility of starting a similar plan for their three children.

The next day turned out to be a self-inflicted red-letter day for Q-T. He was restless after midnight so that he was out of bed earlier than usual. He left home early because he wanted his business to be the first to be tackled by the young manager at the British Bank in the centre of town. After waiting anxiously for about ten long minutes he was ushered into the manager's office. The white man was fully dressed in a dark business suit which matched stitch for stitch the sartorial elegance of Q-T's dark Regent street suit worn over a shiny white starched collar and shirt. The two had met before on another business, therefore they were both at ease. After the exchange of greetings and the usual pleasantries, Q-T narrated his story and presented the envelope containing assorted West African currency notes and coins to the manager. On opening and glancing at the contents, the young manager was truly shocked beyond his self-control, his young face flushed bright red and his normally restrained voice exploded beyond recognition saying,

"Mr Quinton-Taki! A senior lawyer and King's counsel of the High Court of British West Africa! How could you keep such a huge quantity of cash at home and for so long?"

Q-T assumed the defensive posture with his usual court room mode and responded,

"As I told you earlier the money was found in the safe of my late elder brother Jeff who was a successful farmer at Pakro in the hinterland. He died about a year ago and I discovered the money in his safe which was brought down intact from Pakro. He left a lone heir, a daughter who is now 18. The young girl currently is my ward by adoption and fully integrated with my original family. The will of my late brother stated clearly that the money was earmarked for her education up to the tertiary level."

"Your villager brother could be excused for committing the offence for keeping such a large sum at home for several reasons including lack of nearby banking facilities, but for you to do the same for over a year is unacceptable."

"I am very sorry; at least I am here now and as the sages say, 'better late than never'."

Mr Quinton-Taki you are an elderly man, and I should not be so stern, you are forgiven."

Both gentlemen smiled, shook hands and peace was declared.

"How may I help you to regularise the situation?" asked the kind manager.

"I would be grateful if you would kindly engage some of your trusted professionals to sort and count the money and then deposit the amount into a special account with myself and Robyn Quinton-Taki as joint signatories. However, as she is currently underage, I shall be the sole signatory, but when she turns 21 there will be two signatories valid jointly or singly."

"I will do that for you. The account will be securely opened by the close of day, therefore if you pass by tomorrow morning the documentation will only need your signature for completion. The young lady's signature will become necessary when she achieves the age of maturity in 3 years' time. By the way have you any idea of the amount of money in the envelope?"

"Yes of course, good old brother Jeff kept a record of all inputs with dates and comments which you will find in the small notebook enclosed."

"Good, your brother was a very wise man."

James Q-T thanked him profusely and got out quickly from the bank manager's office and the bank building before perchance the good manager changed his mind.

Q-T arrived home at 1.00 pm in very good spirits. From the bank he rushed to the High Court and was able to dispose of two of his difficult cases satisfactorily. He plunged into conversation without waiting for the usual probing questions from his inquisitive but well-meaning wife. He said to his wife,

"I have had a very busy and enormously successful morning; everything went my way. The bank manager was very sympathetic and cooperative. The money is to be counted and deposited in an account and tomorrow by lunch time all the documentation would have been signed, sealed and delivered to me."

"By the way were you aware of the amount of money in that envelope or did you leave it entirely in trust to the manager? "

"Don't be ridiculous, of course I knew the exact amount. Your late brother-in-law Jeff was always the shrewd businessman in the family, he had meticulously documented all cash deposits with dates and appropriate comments regarding target and duly stored the information in the notebook enclosed in the envelope. Although I gave the notebook to the manager which I considered as fair and correct banking procedure, I made sure I wrote the total amount on an official Q-T letter head duly signed and dated and stowed away safely in my safe upstairs."

"Dear husband, I am glad that you are even wiser than your late big brother, but I still have a question; who is or are the signatories of this account?"

"Currently I am the sole signatory. When Robyn attains the maturity age of twenty one, she will become the second signatory."

"Have you dispatched the promised letter to Robyn's maternal aunt as promised or planned?"

"Yes of course, the mail boat is due to depart from our shores on Wednesday and arrive at Port Harcourt in five days. If the good lady realises the urgency and replies immediately, we will surely know the score within a month. Meanwhile we just have to hold tight and keep our fingers crossed. We have communicated our plans to Mrs Eric Wuta's family in Cape Coast to reassure them that we mean to comply with the plans so carefully laid out in Cape Coast. I received a cryptic telegram from Eric thanking us profusely for salvaging his family life."

On looking deeply into the eyes of his dear wife Q-T instinctively felt that there was something still disturbing her. He tactfully persuaded her to state her worry and when she did it was a bombshell.

"I want to know whether you have made similar plans to ensure that our children experience tertiary education in London?"

"I know what is going on in your mind. Let me tell you now that the money in the envelope was amassed by my elder brother who was indeed a very shrewd businessman. It was my choice to stay in town and practice law. You have guessed right, I have not amassed as much wealth as he had but I am quite satisfied with my relative poverty: my late brother's money by his will belongs entirely to Robyn to spend in whatever way she wishes, I refuse to be tempted to touch that money. Dear wife, remember that so long as there is life there is hope, and God willing our children will be educated to the level they deserve."

Mrs Q-T realised at once that in her eagerness to promote her children who now looked poor compared to their very rich cousin Robyn, she had inadvertently upset her good-natured husband. She there and then decided to drop the subject and apologise for her tactless intervention. Q-T accepted her apology and soon everything was forgotten and there was peace.

Six weeks after the above episode the long-expected letter from Calabar arrived and the contents were favourable to their plans. The letter was from Mrs Patti Panford, Robyn's maternal aunt. She would be delighted to look after her own sister's daughter if she eventually decided to come to Calabar. She then reassured them that since her English/Swiss husband died and her only son relocated to London to train as a doctor she had lived alone in their big house on the outskirts of Calabar, surrounded by servants and the workers of her large bakery and that it would be nice to have a close family member as a companion. Q-T was impressed by the letter and decided it must be read by all family members including Robyn. Mrs Q-T was the first to read the letter soon after her husband had left the house for the office. After her first quick reading she felt painful twangs of jealousy and resentment deep in her bosom. Mrs Q-T being aware that the deep-seated resentment she had for the orphan was wrong in the sight of God, resolved to fight it with all her will power to avoid its discovery which would be too embarrassing to bear. On the other hand, her maternal instinct geared solely to the protection and welfare of her own children engendered a conflict deep in her heart and mind. She decided to pray fervently day and night over the issue and hope that the Almighty God himself would eventually come to her rescue. She was put to the test immediately when at that very moment her husband barged in with the news that all family members were elated by the response from Calabar and that preparations were to be hurried so that six and not twelve months would be the waiting time. Mrs Q-T put on a good act pretending to be very happy with the turn of events when really deep down in her heart she did not feel that way.

PREPARATIONS FOR ROBYN'S TRIP TO CALABAR

The telegram from Robyn's aunt confirming her preparedness to receive and sponsor Robyn was the cue which triggered serious preparations towards her impending departure to Nigeria. With that aim in view, Lawyer James Q-T arranged an urgent meeting at her sister's house to plan the way forward. The meeting was attended by old uncle Cobbinah alias Kobby, Q-T himself, Mrs Kate Wuta who was scheduled to become the babysitter, Aunt Debby who was on the famous delegation to Pakro and last but not the least Robyn herself. Mrs Q-T was invited but she declined the invitation for reasons best known to herself and perhaps also to her husband who was slowly beginning to appreciate the deep antipathy his wife harboured for his niece Robyn.

Lawyer Q-T was the first to speak when all were comfortably

seated, and he said,

"Well! You all know why we are here and I thank you all for coming. Our task has been rendered easy by the prompt favourable response we have received from Robyn's aunt. The baby Martha is in good health and is currently breast feeding only. Mother Robyn is also in good health and spirits. My sister Mrs Kate Wuta and her helpers are very fond of the baby and vice versa. The kind midwife who does regular home visits assures us that if bottle feeding is introduced at the age of 6 months, the baby should be fully weaned by the age of 9 months to 1 year, which means that we could be looking at June next year for the departure of Robyn to Calabar. I pause here for your comments."

Uncle Kobby was the next to speak and he said, "We are all anxious to know Robyn's point of view on all these arrangements. After all she is the principal architect and also the beneficiary."

He paused and looked at Robyn who graciously responded thus: "Thank you Uncle Kobby and thank you all for your great concern and great solidarity. Baby Martha and I are doing very well and Aunt Kate has been a pillar of strength always there for us to lean on. The nurse has been very helpful too with her professional advice since she learned about the need for early weaning to enable me embark on the trip to Calabar. She has assured me that six months exclusive breast feeding is ideal for Martha and that even at four months we should start feeding her with a small spoon rather than with the bottle and teat, which although is the European method is far inferior to our native cup and spoon method for several reasons which she has patiently and thoroughly explained to me. I have written to my aunt in Calabar to thank her for her kind offer. Right now, I am eagerly looking forward to my schooling in Calabar where a suitable school for adults has already been identified and enrolment processes initiated by my kind aunt."

"I have a question."

"Uncle Kobby kindly feel free and ask your question." Q-T responded looking straight into the eyes of Kobby.

"Have the details of the financial arrangements been worked out by this family or are we going to depend entirely on charity of Robyn's maternal aunt in Calabar?"

Lawyer James Q-T responded without any hesitation.

"Our late brother had made all the financial arrangements before he died, and I am acting strictly according to his plans. I have already transferred the money into the joint accounts of Robyn Quinton-Taki and James Quinton-Taki at the British West African Bank in Calabar from where all bills regarding this project will be settled under my sole authorisation until Robyn attains the age of 21 and assumes full responsibility for her father's legacy."

Uncle Kobby who was hitherto famous for his reticence at family gatherings waded in most uncharacteristically and said authoritatively,

"Son! You have indeed hit the nail on the head by referring to the idea of 'legacy'. Are you aware that your brother farmed all those years on family land and not on his own land therefore by tradition a certain proportion of the proceeds thereof belonged to the family of the original owner Stonewall Quinton-Taki of blessed memory?"

"Indeed, I am fully aware, after all I was Stonewall's legal representative for several years before he died. The fact is we never bothered to sit down to work out the arithmetic of the proportions of what goes to whom during the lifetime of our brother Jeff and thus allowed him to reckon rightly or wrongly that all belonged to him to dispense according to his wishes. It is a well-known principle of Roman law which we have inherited from the British which says that you cannot give what you do not possess, therefore Uncle you are right, Jeff could not will everything but he could certainly will his part of it. What we must do now is to do what we should have done during his lifetime, and that is to negotiate with his sole heir Robyn who is currently a minor and therefore not a legal entity. The good news is that since I am named in the will as her guardian I can act for her now, but it could be messy if she decides to renegotiate when she attains legal maturity. It is my well-considered opinion that for the interim we should let sleeping dogs lie and let me run the minor Robyn's affairs albeit with family advice and inputs even as we are doing now with fairness and goodwill towards the heir. By doing that there is no doubt in my mind that Jeff's sole heir Robyn will respond positively to the negotiations which would come on in a few years from now. So, Uncle, all is not lost: we are a family, including Robyn, for whose benefit we are gathered here this evening."

"Son, you have analysed the situation very well. I agree with you and I hope all at this meeting will let sleeping dogs lie for now."

Mrs Wuta then signalled that she had something to say.

"Dinner is served; but before we eat, we have one more problem to solve, implying that I agree with all that has transpired so far. Robyn will be only 19 and legally a minor when she embarks on her long overseas journey barely six months from now, besides she is female in this our male dominated society. I feel strongly that she must not travel alone. She must be accompanied by a chaperone preferably an elderly female family member or reliable family friend."

Uncle Kobby responded without delay. "Sister that is very wise of you, I suggest that we incorporate the idea in our plans, factor in the extra expenses and ponder carefully whom to nominate as chaperon and let us do the selection at our next meeting."

At that juncture Q-T, the chairman, closed the meeting and they all trooped in to sample Kate Wuta's dinner.

CHAPTER FIVE

CHRISTMAS TIME 1901

Christmas of 1901 was a happy interlude at the James Quinton-Taki mansion except for one omission: Eric and his family could not participate; indeed, they were deliberately kept out in order to satisfy one of the conditions which facilitated the salvaging of Eric's marriage, namely the physical separation of Eric and Robyn for as long as possible.

Christmas day was spent traditionally as it had always been celebrated in the family since time immemorial. All the children and adults were dressed up in new clothes most of which had been ordered from abroad and taken delivery of only a few weeks before Christmas day. The children had hardly slept a wink since the 24th night fireworks following which there was a party with dance music, lemonade, crunchy sweet biscuits and home-baked cakes for the children on the one hand, and beer, wine and spirits for the adults.

After the obligatory morning church service on Christmas day at the Methodist Cathedral, they all rushed home to welcome the rest of the extended family for the long-awaited sumptuous dinner of roasted turkey, spiced baked yam balls, fried imported bacon and sausage rolls, jollof rice, vegetable and salmon salad garnished with sliced boiled eggs and tasty imported salad creams from England. The menu for the dessert that followed was equally expansive, exciting and exotic consisting of a mixture of local and canned imported fruits, traditional Christmas puddings served with rich cream, fruit cakes and apple tarts and so on...all washed down with the choicest French brandies and Scottish and Irish liquors for the adults and for the children, more lemonade.

After the Christmas lunch all the children trooped to play in the cool spacious veranda on the north side of the house which was pleasant this time of the year as the sun hovered in the south over the tropic of Capricorn. Meanwhile the adults drifted half-drunk to the spacious lounge to continue the celebrations. Nobody felt tired or sleepy despite the heavy four course meal along with the choicest wines. Indeed, there was more to drink as the tables in the hall were fully decorated with beautiful bottles of the best brandies, port, liqueur and even champagnes waiting to be popped for toasts. The conversation flowed freely and the jokes supplied as usual by the witty elders of the family were hilarious and suited the occasion perfectly. Time moved fast under the circumstances and before they were aware it was 4.30 pm, close to the Christmas teatime, which called for another ritual not to be missed at any cost in the Quinton-Taki mansion. Within a twinkle of an eye tea was ready to be served in the choicest custom-made china, accompanied by cakes, sandwiches, and cookies of every description. The enthusiasm with which all and sundry helped themselves reflected the joy of the occasion and the spirit of the season. No sooner had the tea session ended than Uncle Kobby thought it was time to propose a toast to their hosts Mr and Mrs James Quinton-Taki. He called all to attention by gently knocking an empty drinking glass with a teaspoon. All was quiet such that one could hear a pin drop, and that was the cue for Uncle Kobby to start what turned out to be a very brief but brilliant speech from an eloquent old man wearing on this festive day not a European suit but rather a magnificent and elegant kente cloth woven in Bonwire by master craftsmen. He said:

"My dear relatives and friends, bear with me while I say a few words with permission from our kind host and head of this precious family. The real purpose of my speech is to propose a toast but, before I do that, I need to remind you of some history. Although I am the oldest around here, I am not the official head of this family. I was the last born and youngest brother of Stonewall Quinton-Taki whose hard work and vision has revived in modern times this dear family of ours. By the grace of God, he enjoyed a long active and fruitful life and was able to educate and train his younger siblings including myself, my own father having died too early. More importantly my elder brother Stonewall also had several children namely Jeff who was summoned to eternity two years ago, sister Kate who was born three years before her late brother Jeff, James our current host came after Jeff and last but not the least of Papa Stonewall's children the perpetually youthful and beautiful sister Debbie over there. It is important to note that all the members of family I have listed are my nieces and nephews with whom I grew up as peers since we belonged to same age group, indeed I am only eighteen months older than my niece Kate. This brings me to the important historical fact which symbolises the wisdom of our original patriarch, good old Papa Stonewall, father to my nieces and nephews but to me an elder biological brother but at the same time the only functional father I knew. Stonewall was quick to observe the great potential of his second son James at an early age and he carefully nurtured him. He saved the best part of his earnings in order to dispatch him to London to study Law as there were no government scholarships for natives in those days. On the eve of James's departure to London, Papa Stonewall assembled all his children including me in the privacy of his bedroom for a profound policy statement. On that occasion our patriarch Stonewall who unlike me was a man of very few words spoke at length. Time is far spent on this joyous day and therefore I will summarize it in a few sentences. He told us that he had gathered us in the privacy of his bedroom to tell us what we probably knew already plus a few new and very important things. He confirmed that the youngest among us, our brother

James was due to embark on a long voyage to London to study Law and that our brother who had distinguished himself at secondary school in Cape Coast and had matriculated so well that the University of London authorities had offered him a University scholarship. But there was a hitch in that the colonial office had provision for Medicine, Science, Mathematics and even the Arts and Humanities but not for colonial students who wanted to do Law. By the grace of God Stonewall had anticipated the problem when he was preparing the mind of our brother James to pursue Law and had saved enough money to sponsor the trip to London, hoping that the University would honour its promise of the scholarship to cover tuition if not travel and boarding fees. Stonewall proudly boasted that he had already transferred the entire funds to cover all expenses for the initial LLB degree and the subsequent professional Law courses at Gray's Inn. In short, he assured us that our young brother would return to Accra in a few years a fully qualified Lawyer. We all applauded but only for a very brief moment because he aggressively truncated the applause and rebuked us for rudely interrupting him because the best was yet to be revealed. He started the bombshell with two quotations, the first a famous proverb of the Ga people "Onukpa taashi ni awuo gbeke Mantse" meaning the eldest may be superseded by the youngest in the selection of a Chief." And the second from the holy Bible "The first shall be the last, and the last first." He further explained that he was communicating his decision that it was his well-considered wish that our young brother should be accepted as the future head of the family and that his tenure would start on the day of his arrival from London as a fully qualified Lawyer, whether he Stonewall was alive or not, implying that he was prepared to step aside for James. He prayed to the Almighty God to let him live to witness that day. The agreement to his suggestion was spontaneous and unanimous. By the grace of God Stonewall lived to witness Lawyer James's return from London and he officially handed the headship of the family to him. James served us with distinction for many years before Stonewall died and as I am sure you will all agree he has continued to be very good to and for us. His recent elevation to the Legislative Council made the family proud. With his and your permission let me pop this champagne.

"Now let us charge our glasses, raise them high, and then drink to the health, wealth, and long life of our illustrious family head, may he live long to see his grand and great grandchildren!"

The applause was loud and spontaneous and they all sang *For He Is A Jolly Good Fellow* several times then there was silence, the cue for him to respond to the splendid toast so ably proposed by his uncle Kobby. James, already standing, surveyed the familiar and friendly audience from left to right, took a deep breath in with the characteristic broad smile and said,

"Although I cannot match the brilliant oratory of my dear uncle Kobby, I am obliged to say something lest I breach protocol, an inexcusable offence not to be tolerated in civilized society. I must first and foremost thank the Almighty God for giving us this Christmas day and enabling us to celebrate so joyously. Secondly, I wish to thank my uncle and our oldest and very learned relative for giving us a priceless insight of our history and also proposing that magnificent toast to my health. Finally, I thank all of you for gracing the occasion and singing so graciously for me. The principal hostess of the occasion is of course my wife, ably assisted by our growing up children and the household staff; on behalf of the family, I sincerely thank all of them. Let us all continue to enjoy ourselves thoroughly through the rest of the season and await the new year when we will meet again and plan and propose resolutions to guide us in the new year with great expectations."

NEW YEAR 1902

The New Year was welcomed in the usual manner by songs of praise and prayers of thanks giving to God in all churches from 10 pm to 11.55 pm, joyous singing and more high-spirited prayers led by the Bishops and Superintendent Ministers to actually usher in the New Year at 12 midnight 1st January 1902, fireworks and open jubilations in the parks and finally champagne popping amid beer, wine, and spirituous drinking parties far into the early morning of the first day of the New Year which fortunately has always been a holiday in the Gold Coast Colony despite vigorous attempts in the past by the imperialists to make it an ordinary working day as it has always been in Europe.

Traditionally, New Year's Day was the day reserved for resolutions, be they private, secret, collective or open.

On this particular New Year's Day, the family assembled at the James Quinton-Taki mansion resolved to bring to a closure the hitherto harrowing scandal at least temporarily by dispatching Robyn to her aunt to pursue her general education in Calabar and then the Law studies in London. They made this resolution boldly and without scruple well knowing that same was the resolve of Robyn. They went further and discussed all the logistics and took important decisions. The first important issue was raised by Kate who reminded them once again that the voyage to Port Harcourt was a long one, lasting at least three days, which meant that passengers would spend three holiday-like nights on board the luxurious ocean liner full of a mixture of black and white revellers, some having been on the boat for 2 weeks and all the way from Liverpool. She had experienced the atmosphere a long time ago when she did a round duty trip with her late husband.

"All who have had similar experiences in the past would no doubt agree with me that it is not a journey to be undertaken alone by a 19-year-old single beautiful girl like Robyn; in other words, she must be accompanied by an elderly matron to act as her chaperon and I nominate our sister Debby for that assignment."

After the brilliant intervention by good old aunt Kate there was absolute silence for several moments; implying that guidance was needed and alerting the head of family that he needed to lead the discussion which he did as follows:

"Dear relatives I am sure you all agree with me that we are indeed lucky to have such a wise woman as a relative. I personally agree with everything she has said including her nomination of sister Debbie as the chaperon. Knowing my sister Kate, I would not be surprised if she has already spoken to and obtained the consent of sister Debbie."

He paused and looked at both sisters, eyeball-to-eyeball, one after the other. Both sisters nodded the affirmative thus giving him the cue to continue. Always quick to avoid being labelled autocratic, the shrewd lawyer looked into the faces of all the relatives and invited comments for or against or alternative to the proposition. The agreement was loud emphatic and most importantly unanimous. He then continued:

"Since I can vouch that adequate funds are available, thanks to the foresight of our late brother, I hope I have your consent to make the firm travel arrangements for Robyn and her aunt Debbie. There is a passenger ocean liner due to leave Accra port in mid-August 1902 and they will be booked cabin class on that boat. For Robyn it will have to be a one-way trip and for sister Debbie, a round trip. Sister Debbie will do the return voyage alone, she will not need a chaperon!"

VOYAGE TO CALABAR

The final resolutions and definite plans for Robyn's trip to Calabar, South Eastern Nigeria having been fully laid down on New Year's Day, the period from January to end of July 1902 was earmarked for implementation on a self-imposed strict time frame. Lawyer James the head of family in a quiet moment in the privacy of his office created a check list and started working on it without delay. He confirmed the booking on the passenger boat and actually selected a cabin with two comfortable beds in the first-class section of *M.V. Accra*, the flagship of Elder Dempster Lines which was scheduled to sail from the Accra port on August 5th, 1902. A good 7 months from the day of departure, he paid for and collected the tickets himself in order to avoid mishaps which often in the past had occurred and naive passengers had lost their bookings to wealthy merchants prepared to bribe the white booking officers.

He rushed to his sister's house from the Elder Dempster office. He arrived there at 12 noon in an excited mood and called as soon as he reached the front door: "Hi! Sister I am here."

"What brings you here when you should be on your way home for lunch?"

"Oh! Nothing much, I am just in my one of those go! go! go! Moods. Seriously, sister, I have just compiled a check list for our project and I need to verify things rather quickly. I have just come from Elder Dempster lines where I not only confirmed the date of Robyn's trip but also paid for the tickets of the two travellers and even went further to select a first-class cabin for them. I am here to inform you that the next few items on the check list will need your serious interventions."

"Brother, I am all ears and ready to also go! go! go! After all we are birds of a feather, equally hyperactive since childhood."

"Sister, for your assignment I need to purchase three portmanteaus at Miller's stores, two large ones for Robyn, and a medium sized one for sister Debbie-Anne. Your duty will be to fill the large portmanteaus with a comprehensive wardrobe of clothing for Robyn's travel and initial stay in her new abode, and the medium-sized portmanteau with appropriate clothing for the short round trip of your sister. Take your time, talk to the beneficiaries and ascertain their needs, tastes or preferences. At the same time remember that you are in charge; make sure you get value for money. Talking about money, endeavour to prepare a budget for the items you decide to purchase 'ready-made' or those you intend to make in your own 'factory'. After you have done that, let me know the amount of money involved and I will withdraw the cash from the bank."

"Brother! Incidentally, what are some of the other items on your so-called check list?"

"Most of them such as letters and telegrams to Robyn's aunt, vaccination of the travellers, financial arrangements at banks in Accra and Calabar, pocket money for the travellers and so on do not concern you; except perhaps the inspection of Pakro farms and trips to Sekondi and Cape coast for obvious reasons."

"I am willing to go and visit Eric in Sekondi any time; as for Pakro, the one trip last year is enough for me. The trip was very tiring if not even dangerous for a middle-aged woman like me. Please count me out of the Pakro trip as well as the Cape Coast one. We have pampered Eric's in-laws too much. It is high time we left them alone."

"Really big Sister, I am disappointed in you because I recollect clearly that the last time we discussed the farm you agreed strongly with Uncle Kobby that we must all be interested in the farm now that brother Jeff is gone to eternity otherwise we might lose it to strangers especially that crafty upstart of a caretaker."

"I still stand by that argument but that does not mean that I am the one to do that type of work, entailing difficult trips to the bush several times a year. After all I am only a woman and a frail middle-aged one at that. You men should look after the family properties in the hinterland and allow us women to concentrate on those in the city."

"Sister Kate you are not frail; you are strong in body and also very energetic, you are the perfect chip of the old block of good old Stonewall Quinton-Taki."

"The flattery will not work this time; I will not change my mind."

"Time will tell."

"The stubbornness will not get you anywhere this time, I am determined to stick to my guns," she retorted, and that brought the conversation to an end with both of them fully aware that the topic would come up again.

James rushed home with mixed feelings, knowing that opposition from his wife on these matters to the benefit of Robyn would be far fiercer than what he had just encountered from his sister. On arrival at home, he was welcomed warmly by his wife and children who had expected him home an hour earlier for lunch. He was so happy with the reception that he decided to defer all talk about the impending travel plans, he opted for a good lunch free of all controversial discussions likely to generate indigestion. Lunch was good, it was followed by the usual afternoon nap and then office work in town.

He had only two clients with relatively minor problems to interview and soon work was over, and he had the whole afternoon to read or write or just meditate over domestic problems: he chose the last option. It dawned on him that he alone was displaying too much enthusiasm over preparations for the forthcoming trip of Robyn to Nigeria. He suspected that he was beginning to bore and alienate those who mattered to him most in life namely his wife, children and sisters who all probably felt that he was paying too much attention to the problems created by Robyn. After all what was at stake was really just the rehabilitation of a naughty girl who had been plunged into trouble by her own mature, adult and legally married uncle who should have known better. What Eric did was obviously illegal on two important counts. First of all, he had carnal knowledge of a minor under 18 years of age which was definitely a criminal offence in Britain, the whole of Europe and even on the American continent.

"In all the places mentioned above I am sure such a crime attracts a custodial sentence without the option of a fine, which means that were we domiciled in any of those places, Eric would be languishing in prison by now. I wonder whether he himself or his mother or his wife are aware of that. Secondly a sexual act involving close relatives, in this case cousins, is definitely incest in all societies including even ours, the only rider is that whereas in our setting it is frowned upon or considered a taboo because of its tendency to generate abnormal babies, it is not considered a crime punishable by a fine or imprisonment. In other jurisdiction incest is a crime and Eric would have faced prosecution. "

During the above quiet meditation, James suddenly realised the basis of the resentment his relatives had been communicating to him as a result of his displaying too much enthusiasm over Robyn's affairs and especially his obsession with the problems surrounding her impending trip to Nigeria. James, being very wise and at the same time humble to a fault, suddenly felt that he had offended his wife and to a lesser extent his sister Kate by his lack of sensitivity. There and then he resolved that henceforth he would be reticent on all affairs concerning Robyn. He would not volunteer any information on the subject but would endeavour to pursue the project quietly to a successful end. If anybody asked him a question as regards progress, he would answer with a few abrupt words nonchalantly. If no questions were asked, he would wait patiently and announce the day of departure perhaps two to three days prior to the event. In the next few days, it became obvious that his assessment of the situation was right, in that nobody including his wife, children, sister and even inquisitive uncle Kobby asked about the affairs of Robyn. Furthermore, he noted that his relationship with all of them remained amazingly cordial in contrast to the period when the only subject he brought in their company was Robyn. He thanked God that he had made the right analysis and taken the right decisions for his own sake and for the sake of Robyn who needed love and attention rather than resentment from her own family members. The prevailing general reticence facilitated tranquillity and swift passage of time so that soon it was mid-July and departure time for Robyn was well and truly imminent.

Lawyer James had wisely shelved the trips to Pakro Farms, Cape Coast and Sekondi for obvious reasons. There was no occasion for an argument with his sister. The only sensitive moment was when the caretaker and manager of the Pakro Farms under his own initiative and without invitation or prompting from James appeared in Accra and informed James that he felt he must give an account of the state of the business at Pakro. The meeting took place in James's office in town, deliberately removed from both the immediate and extended families. Collins the farm manager brought very good news. The overall yield from the farm had been good, especially the returns for palm oil and sugar cane which were record high. The food stuffs such as maize, cassava, plantain and cocoyam had also done very well; the only disappointment was with the farm animals. Some strange disease had attacked the sheep and goats killing many of them before the disease was brought under control thanks to the very efficient veterinary officer who came all the way from Accra to help. Collins dutifully brought all the books and cash from the sales to Accra because there was no safe on the farm any more since the last directive which led to its transfer to Accra. The late owner of the farm never kept an account in the local Post Office Bank because he did not trust that bank. He did not trust that bank because there had been too many occasions in the past when money had disappeared from the so-called strong rooms of Post Office banks countrywide due to straight forward thievery by naughty greedy postmasters who craftily came out after serving relatively short sentences to enjoy their ill-acquired gains without shame. After checking the books and counting the large amount of cash, James paid the farm manager all salaries and allowances due to him plus a handsome bonus which was well appreciated by the faithful farm manager. They finished the business in the office at 12 noon, early enough to go the Bank of British West Africa to deposit the large sum of money. Having completed the bank business, James relaxed and asked Collins to accompany him home for lunch, perfectly aware that it was an opportunity to re-visit the subject of Robyn's intending departure without displaying too much enthusiasm as it were using the Pakro farm manager's visit as a decoy. The first stage of this clever strategy would of course be a call at Kate's house accompanied by Collins. As usual his sister was very pleased to see him and welcomed him in the usual very friendly manner.

"Hi! Brother" she exclaimed when she set eyes on her brother.

"What brings you here on a Friday afternoon? What a pleasant surprise being accompanied by Farm Manager Collins, who is welcome too. Is it a case of the mountain coming to Mohamed rather than the other way round?"

"So, sister, you still remember my original proposal that you were to travel to Pakro Farms to oversee the business there every now and then."

"How can I forget when you were so persistent that we quarrelled vehemently resulting in you shutting me out of your plans completely up till to-day."

"I did not. I rather realised I was being unreasonable with my over enthusiasm about the affairs of Robyn and that I was upsetting everybody including my own wife and children and even Uncle Kobby. Suffice it to say that I am now here with very good news from Pakro Farms. The yield has been very good this year. Farm manager brought a lot of money which we have already deposited at BBWA. He is in a hurry to go back to Pakro, but I thought he deserved lunch so I am taking him home and it was only natural that we stopped over here to say hello. We will discuss the details of the good news Collins brought from Pakro on another occasion."

"Brother before you go, I have a little business to transact with you. Remember you gave me an important assignment."

"Yes of course! I was wondering when I would hear from you."

"Well, you will hear from me now and it will only take a few minutes of your precious time, please come to my room for a moment and I will show you the goods."

Brother and sister left Collins on the veranda and went through the lounge then into Kate's bedroom. James immediately sighted the suitcases all shut and bursting at the seams placed neatly at the far corner of the room. James discerned at once that the suitcases, all obviously loaded to the brim with clothes, represented the fulfilment of the important assignment he had challenged his sister with several months ago. She opened the large suitcases first and displayed Robyn's wardrobe of clothes and other paraphernalia assembled to satisfy all the needs of a well brought up young woman. James was impressed and he thanked his sister profusely.

"You need not thank me much, after all I have just done my duty as it were emulating our noble head of family who never fails to discharge his duties with fervency and zeal."

"Enough of that flattery lest I became swollen headed and lose focus." James playfully retorted.

Next, Kate dutifully opened the third and smallest suitcase and displayed the clothing and items she had put together for her sister's short trip. Equally impressed with the contents of the third, James, although he had budgeted carefully became apprehensive of a prohibitive bill; nevertheless, he kept his anxiety well-hidden and asked his sister coolly,

"How much do I owe you for the lot? You were supposed to tell me the cost before proceeding with the actual purchase, but never mind, the merchandise looks very good and I will comply with whatever you say."

"The ones I made in my shop are free, you may consider them as my contribution to the 'war effort'. I have receipts for the things from the white man's shop and the total amount you owe is £5, ten shillings and six-pence."

"My initial fear was obviously misplaced. The actual amount is well within the budget. I will settle the bill plus a little amount as expenses at our next meeting."

"No, brother; you will not pay any expenses. You are just trying cleverly to compensate me for what I deemed my 'war effort'."

On the way to his mansion with his guest James saw a chance to find out what sort of man Collins really was; firstly, to be sure that he was worthy of a dinner with the family, and secondly to decide how to relate to him on future occasions. Collins passed the interview with flying colours. He was obviously well educated by local standards. Indeed, he was a fully trained schoolteacher and on the verge of becoming a headmaster when the late Jeffery Quinton-Taki enticed him to quit his job to work full-time as farm manager and financial controller of the whole estate at a salary four times what he earned as a teacher, plus free accommodation and free access to farm products. Collins, against all opposition from employers, family and friends enthusiastically took up the appointment at Jeff's Pakro Farms ten years ago and he had not regretted that move. He had been a loyal and efficient worker who never ceased to read widely about farm administration and financial management. He also joined his boss to take overseas correspondence courses in tropical crop production and animal husbandry from reputable Agricultural Colleges in India, Brazil and the Caribbean. Being a trained teacher by profession he learned new facts with ease and was ever ready to teach the farm workers new methods. Even more importantly Jeff realised that Collins was an honest man worth cultivating as a friend and business partner. On arrival at home, he introduced him favourably to his wife. Mrs. Quinton-Taki who had always trusted and respected her husband's skills at judgement of the human character naturally did not hesitate to accept Collins as a good man. Collins sat at table with the family and displayed impeccable table manners which he had obviously acquired at the Methodist Teacher Training College he attended as a young man several years ago. After the sumptuous meal he thanked and said goodbye to the family before he embarked on the long journey back to Pakro.

CHAPTER SIX

FINAL COUNTDOWN TO DEPARTURE TIME FOR ROBYN

Lawyer James Q-T was alone sitting at his desk in his Law office in Victoriaborg near the Accra High Court. It was a Friday. He looked at the calendar on his desk and noted that the date was 18th of July 1902, precisely 18 days before the scheduled day of Robyn's departure on the *M.V. Accra* to Port Harcourt. The luxurious passenger boat was due to sail from Accra port at exactly 6.00 pm on Monday 4th August 1902. Earlier that morning he had received a visitor from Elder Dempster Lines. He was profoundly depressed by the information he received from the visitor whose high rank at Elder Dempster Lines obviously signified the importance of the message. The white officer apologised profusely that they should have informed him earlier but the junior clerk in charge of the file overlooked the problem which only came to the attention of the manager the previous day, necessitating the rush to his office without prior warning. Apparently, the company had introduced a new rule about 6 months earlier that women aged between 18 and 40 needed to be accompanied by an adult or elderly gentleman before they could travel in the first- or second-class passenger areas of the boat. Ironically had they been travelling third class where passengers were accommodated in large common dormitories, they could travel unaccompanied. The rule was engendered from a few scandals which surfaced when unaccompanied women were indecently assaulted by male passengers and on one occasion by a daring crew member.

When James finally realized that the rule could not be circumvented, it became necessary to find a solution because abandoning the trip was not an option to be entertained. The white man assured him that the shipping company was prepared to go to any length to accommodate the extra passenger even at this late stage because without him the two women could not travel on the Elder Dempster ship. James assured the white officer that the rule will be obeyed, and a suitable elderly gentleman will accompany the two women. When the white man left his office the full effect of the message hit him. He remained glued to his chair and meditated intensely in search of a solution to this entirely new and peculiar problem. Suddenly the solution emerged. Uncle Kobby came to mind as the most suitable person; if that failed then it would have to be himself. However, he was too busy and preoccupied with very important cases to attend to especially as the law courts' annual vacation was due to start in less than six weeks. He resolved to use all his persuasive skills to induce Uncle Kobby to take on this unexpected assignment. With his mind thus made up, he rushed out of his office with the aim of confronting his uncle at his home before lunchtime. However, barely halfway to his intended destination, he changed his mind on realising that in such delicate matters it was always best to seek clearance or advice from the women first. He therefore changed direction and hurried instead to his sister Kate's house.

James arrived at his sister's house at about 12.30 pm. On seeing him she exclaimed, "Brother! What are you doing here when you are expected at your mansion for lunch by your good wife? There is no doubt in my mind that you have an important business to transact."

"I have come straight from my office following an unusual visitation from the white assistant manager of the local office of Elder Dempster Lines. There is a problem. Apparently unaccompanied women aged 18 to 40 cannot travel cabin or first class on their boats because of recent assaults on some of them by male fellow passengers and sometimes by crew members. The management of Elder Dempster Lines reckon that our two booked passengers fall into that category and they must therefore be accompanied by an adult male escort."

He paused, but Kate beckoned him to carry on talking.

"Well, I intend to persuade Uncle Kobby to do that, but first of all I need your advice just in case there is a better or more appropriate option I have overlooked."

"I quite remember those scandals which occurred on the boats especially that they always happened along this west coast of Africa. I agree with the Elder Dempster Lines, our men sometimes behave like animals on long boat journeys. On your choice of Kobby as escort I concur, there can be no better choice, and I sincerely hope that he consents to do the job."

"Sister, I implore you to inform Debby and to see to it that she agrees to the change, if not we are doomed. Elder Dempster Lines has assured me that they will provide passage for the escort at a discount."

"Good show! I will persuade or rather convince her to accept the new arrangement and let you know early to-morrow morning."

"That will be perfect because the Elder Dempster office opens on Saturdays up to 12 noon, so as soon as I get clearance from you, I will go there to finalise the new arrangement. Bear in mind that today is the 18th of July, and the boat is due to sail at 6.00 pm on the 4th of August. We have just over two weeks to D-day."

"Never mind brother! We shall overcome."

"I sincerely hope so."

With that final remark, James rushed to his mansion for the

belated Friday lunch.

By sheer coincidence, Uncle Kobby had already arrived at the mansion for lunch, having a standing invitation which he very rarely honoured. James decided that it would be strategic to discuss the matters arising from the Elder Dempster Lines visitation with his wife and uncle over the pre-lunch beer. He announced that they should assemble at the study for a small conference. The summoned instinctively knew that the matter would concern Robyn's travel arrangements which James had been reticent about for too long. The information he produced was totally unexpected and the two listeners were dumbfounded. Both, however, remembered the assault scandals which had thoroughly shocked civil society a few years ago, but were not aware that Elder Dempster had instituted such drastic measures to prevent future occurrences. The silence was broken by James with the following words:

"Well, Uncle Kobby, it has to be either myself or you, since I cannot think of anyone else capable of such a task. I hereby plead that I have some rather important cases coming up, and although I know that your business commitments are equally important, I would be very grateful if you would kindly take up this assignment."

There was another long pause which was eventually broken by Mrs Q-T.

"Uncle Kobby, it is my humble plea that you try to take up this job for the sake of the family. James cannot do it for several reasons, and he should be candid enough to beg you to do the job."

It was Uncle Kobby's turn to speak and he obliged with a question.

"How long will it take the *M.V. Accra* to do the round-trip Accra-Calabar-Accra?"

"Eight days, all things being normal. The longest in recent history was 14 days and that was under extreme and unusual circumstances."

"I am impressed that you have already done that research. I am sure my business assistants can manage two weeks without me."

James was quick to ask: "Does that mean that you will do the assignment?"

Uncle Kobby answered with an emphatic "Yes."

There was instant relief and with that problem solved they went for a good lunch.

On the same afternoon that the above discussion took place, but on the other side of town, Mrs Kate Wuta assembled her younger sister Debbie and Robyn in the privacy of her bedroom for a travel briefing. She first of all narrated the latest information she had gathered from her brother at length and in great detail, including the fact that Uncle Kobby was to escort them to Port Harcourt in compliance with the rule. She spoke authoritatively, leaving the two prospective travellers with no room to express opinions or dissent. Robyn was in no position to object, and Mrs Wuta's influence over her younger sister had always been such that, when important issues arose, she always had her way, therefore it was not surprising that Debby just accepted everything as a fait accompli.

The meeting ended well. Debbie went home to complete her packing and to contemplate the implication of a whole week of sea trip not only with her affable niece Robyn but also with her elderly uncle Kobby who on 'good' days could be even more affable than Robyn.

LOW PROFILE DEPARTURE TO PORT HARCOURT

The morning of the departure finally arrived. It was the 4th of August and a fine sunny morning with faint seasonal clouds on the horizon with no threat of storms or rain thus assuring a quiet normal embarkation throughout the day. Uncle Kobby, accompanied by James, was the first Quinton–Taki to embark at 3.00 pm when the Accra port was very quiet. He went through the formalities without any hitch and was led to his first-class cabin, a good-sized L-shaped apartment with a well-dressed double bed, wardrobe, dressing table and a small writing desk all in the right wing of the room whose mid portion was occupied by a small door which opened into a bathroom with a bathtub, washbasin and water closet. The smaller left wing of the room formed the entrance lobby and the sitting room. The two gentlemen sat in comfortable armchairs at the far corner of the sitting room. There was also a two-seater sofa placed under the porthole overlooking the starboard side of the boat. Arranged on the low table in the middle of the sitting room were four shiny glasses on a tray. On the other side of the table were placed unopened bottles of Portuguese port, Scottish Whisky, French brandy and an assortment of English sodas and lemonades. There was also a flask of cold water, a basket of assorted tropical and temperate fruits labelled with a beautiful courtesy 'Welcome to *M.V. Accra*' card. The gentlemen served themselves with generous portions of port, said 'cheers' then took sips of the drink followed by snippets of fruit and small chops on the table. They indulged in small talk interspersed with short periods of serious discussions on their immediate current affairs. At 4.30 pm they left the cabin and climbed to the entrance deck; where Robyn and her two aunts who had just been lifted off the surf boat onto the deck were standing. An hour earlier Robyn and her 45-year-old aunt Debbie and Mrs Quinton-Taki had finished dressing and said their goodbyes to the several family members who had gathered at the Q-T mansion to see them off. The departure goodbyes were not easy to accomplish especially for Robyn who knew that she was not going to see her baby Martha for the next several years, may be eight to ten years by which time she would be almost grown up with a mind and character of her own and totally devoid of anything to do with her mother Robyn. Robyn wept uncontrollably while the baby Martha totally oblivious to the true state of affairs rejoiced at seeing her mother and great aunt Debbie so well and colourfully dressed. Naturally, the ladies arrived on deck in a very subdued if not depressed mood. James and Uncle Kobby however noticing the obvious depression did their best to cheer them up. After the completion of the embarkation formalities, the gentlemen accompanied the ladies to their first-class cabin which was only a few doors away from Uncle Kobby's on the same corridor. The manager himself was around, apologising profusely, saying that he tried to put them in adjacent cabins but in vain. James was at his gentlemanly best for the occasion and rather thanked the manager on behalf of the whole family for his effort.

The ladies' cabin was an exact replica of uncle Kobby's except that it was a mirror image so that as they entered the cabin objects to the right were to the left in Uncle Kobby's cabin. The gentlemen had difficulty adjusting, but for the ladies everything looked perfect. The ladies looked round, placed their belongings in the appropriate drawers and shelves, then came to join the gentlemen in the sitting room. James and Uncle Kobby had some more port while the ladies settled for lemonade and fruits. At exactly 5.30 pm a loud bell rang, and it was announced that all visitors must leave the boat and hurry onto the boats in order to be taken ashore. Things happened quickly and soon James and his wife were waving goodbye and wishing the voyagers safe sailing and safe landing at Port Calabar. While on the boat going to the beach Mrs Q-T whispered into her husband's ear, "I wish we were travelling."

James immediately responded; "Really! Where do you wish to go?"

She replied without hesitation: "The USA of course."

"Why USA, and why of course?"

"Because you have been there before, and I have not."

"It was a business trip and the business partners paid for me."

"I have been told that if you had insisted, they would have paid for me to accompany you."

"Who told you that? Well to a certain extent the company would have paid but remember that at that time we had three young children including a baby who needed breastfeeding."

"Yes, I know, but now that all the children are grown up, I am ready for a trip to the USA."

The boat eventually reached the shore and they disembarked. Mark the driver was waiting for them with the horse and carriage. They hopped on the vehicle, and soon they were back home at the mansion where the whole family had assembled waiting for them. They described how beautiful the interior of the boat was and all the children expressed the wish that next time they must also be given the chance to see the interior decor of a passenger boat and if possible be given the opportunity to travel far away.

The *M. V. Accra* moved at first slowly, then gathered momentum.

All the passengers seemed to be leaning dangerously over the deck railings trying to identify their friends and loved ones standing far ashore and also waving frantically. Soon the shore was beyond the horizon and they knew they had well and truly departed from the Gold Coast colony. The travellers with weak inner ear balancing systems started suffering from sea and motion sickness and had to be rushed into their cabins to lie down. The three Q-T travellers fortunately did not suffer from this early sea sickness and therefore managed to stroll leisurely to the lounge. A loud bell tolled, and it was announced that dinner would be served at 6.30 pm, passengers were however advised to go to the dining room a few minutes earlier to identify the tables which had been allocated to them. They were free to choose alternate tables if they wished particularly to be with some particular loved ones or friends. Robyn and her aunt went to their cabin to freshen up for dinner, while Uncle Kobby went directly to the dining room where he was pleasantly surprised that management had chosen a nice table for them, almost next to the Captain's table. There were six places on that table. Apart from the Q-T family members, the remaining places had been allocated to Mr Bandile an elderly Lagosian businessman stationed at Agona Swedru and his two teenage daughters. They were apparently on their way to Calabar to visit the family of the late Mrs Bandile who had died tragically at Swedru and been buried there. Two years had enabled their grief to heal sufficiently so that they were not unduly depressed. Uncle Kobby was already on good conversational terms with the Bandile family when Robyn and her aunt arrived.

Although dinner was very formal as expected in any first-class dining room on a British luxury passenger liner and consisted of several courses with appropriate wines for soup, main dish, desert, coffee and biscuits etc, the Q-T family members, thanks to the lifestyle they had been exposed to at the famous Q-T mansion in Accra felt comfortable and at home. Robyn was grateful that she had been allowed to get used to such formal occasions by the generosity and magnanimity of Mr and Mrs James Quinton-Taki, notwithstanding the little push from her own bosom friend Eric who had instigated the change from eating with the servants in the kitchen to eating at table with the entire family. Robyn noticed that the Bandile girls were far from being at ease and indeed had to depend heavily on their father for instructions at every stage of the dinner in order to apply the correct table manners. Dinner lasted about 50 minutes. When it was over, they all proceeded to the magnificent and chandelier-lit first-class lounge for more coffee and brandy for those who so desired. Uncle Kobby was in a good mood and he enjoyed himself thoroughly aided and abetted fully by the happy go lucky Mr Bandile. The girls retired to their cabins early leaving the adults to continue the reverie well towards midnight. Bandile amused Debbie and Kobby tremendously with great stories gathered from his hotel business at Agona Swedru deep in the forest of the Eastern province of the Gold Coast. When Bandile finally departed the scene, Uncle Kobby and Debby reminisced about old times.

Kobby remarked that it was nearly 20 years ago that he had to terminate their secret friendship rather suddenly because he suspected that they were being monitored by some nosey family members and friends.

“But here we are now after so many years in the wilderness of self-imposed abstention and I sincerely feel as though nothing has changed, I do not know about you.”

She did not respond immediately to Kobby’s remarks. The sages have always known that when consummation is desired equally by both parties and the venue and or timing become problematic the ladies usually have the knack of coming up with a solution, and it was exactly so on this occasion. Debbie sensed that Kobby still had feelings for her, and she knew herself well enough to realise that the feeling was mutual. She broke the ice by suggesting the following:

"I think it is too late for us to be seen sitting here; let us go to your room and talk there."

Kobby was quick to concur. So, to his room they virtually rushed and as soon as they were seated in the privacy of Kobby's cabin Debbie was the first to speak.

"You said something in the lounge, which is not quite true, that you alone and not together with me took the decision to terminate our relationship."

"My dearest Debbie, the truth is that we never really had the chance to discuss what was then an emergency. I was afraid that your naughty cousin Eric who was 10 years old at that time had seen too much. You remember that on one occasion he caught us almost red-handed, literally pants down. Our only reprieve was that it was dark in the room and he was not quite sure that it was you or another woman he saw on the couch with me. Be it as it may, he reported to his mother that he saw me playing 'naughty' games on the couch with a woman who resembled Aunt Debbie. Your sister Kate questioned me, but I of course denied vehemently and advised her strongly to reprimand her son for delving into adult affairs. I there and then banned Eric from going to my house uninvited and making sure he knocked before entering. Did Kate question you on that occasion?"

"Yes, she did, and I also denied vehemently and tearfully. She apologised and added that she was never going to refer to that episode again."

Romance in the cabin of the steamer

"And did you believe her? I did not, indeed I suspected strongly that she rather continued to watch the two of us closely for clues and even went further to engage professional spies to monitor our movements. That is why I presented you with the decision that we must terminate our relationship at once. I dare say that we have been clever and resolute over the years such that all clues suggestive of the affair were thoroughly obliterated. The proof that nobody suspects us is this trip. Let us have a drink to that."

Kobby poured himself a good portion of brandy and the same measure of port for Debbie. They took long sips and became tipsy. They started kissing each other passionately on the couch just like the old times again and again. They bundled each other to the bedroom where the lovemaking continued for a long time to the utter amazement of both partners. Kobby remarked that at 65 he thought he was finished with these youthful games and indeed though he had tried on several occasions in the recent times he had not been successful and obviously the credit today belonged to the exquisite beauty and attractiveness Debbie exuded at the mature age of 45. Debbie suddenly remembered why she was on the boat – to chaperon Robyn and prevent such romantic games being visited on her by total strangers. It was therefore ironic that she Debbie had proven to be the naughty one on the very first night. The two lovers dressed quickly and rushed out to check on the 'safety' of Robyn. On arrival, Debbie tried opening the cabin door without knocking! She gave a sigh of relief when she noted that the door was not only locked but securely bolted on the inner side. She then knocked and there was a cautious response. "Who is it?" Robyn asked. Debbie then answered softly: "It is me, Debbie".

While waiting for Robyn to come and unlock and unbolt the door, Debbie signalled Kobby to stand well back and out of the view of Robyn. As soon as the door was about to be opened, she signalled Uncle Kobby to go away which he did quickly and without protesting, so that as far as Robyn could discern, Debbie was unaccompanied. Robyn pretended to be half asleep and therefore not ready for conversation: she rather curled up into the cosy bed to continue the faked blissful sleep while in reality she was speculating on the possible nocturnal escapades of her beautiful vivacious aunt and one or perhaps both fine gentlemen she had been with all night.

Robyn's youthful and super libidinous imagination was further charged when Debbie removed her clothes, rushed to the bathroom for a cold shower, changed into night clothes and then hopped into the cosy bed. She instinctively knew that her aunt had been involved in some adult games; but with whom? The entire scenery reminded her of her torrid escapades with Eric and all her loving tissues became pleasantly stiff, inviting self-touching which she resisted with all the willpower she could muster under the circumstances. She finally managed to fall asleep long after her romantic aunt had done same.

The two ladies woke up the following morning to note that the boat was stationary and securely anchored at Lagos Harbour. However, disembarkation had not started. They went for breakfast at 8.00 am and at exactly 8.30 am disembarkation started. Uncle Kobby was keen to go ashore and explore the city of Lagos but Debbie and Robyn decided to relax in their cabin. Lagos being a very busy port, and their cabin being at the port side of the boat, they could view through the portholes all that was happening in the harbour. Robyn was intrigued and amused by the beehive-like activities of the port workers, and the pomposity and caricature-like vanity of the disembarking

Lagosians after their stay in Europe. She was equally amused by the elaborately dressed new passengers and visitors who obviously considered the occasion as an important one way beyond her imagination, bearing in mind that their destination was near-by Calabar.

Debbie and Robyn had practically the whole day to themselves to talk on a wide range of topics and thereby become better acquainted with each other. They soon realised how similar they were. The friendly atmosphere enabled them to probe each other's personality and past emotional histories. Robyn for the first time learned about how Debbie's two previous marriages had failed because of her inability to produce children because of repeated spontaneous abortions when her pregnancies were three to four months old. Debbie confessed to her niece that she had at last achieved a peace of mind after accepting that she was destined to be a life-long childless spinster. Robyn disagreed and vehemently admonished her not to give up praying for a miracle. Robyn attempted to cheer up her aunt by saying:

"You never know, this very trip may be the breakthrough miracle. I have noticed that Mr Bandile is in love with you, the poor guy is unable to hide his feelings, I wonder whether old uncle Kobby has noticed?"

"Robyn! You are indeed precocious, no doubt that is how you got involved with your naughty playboy cousin Eric."

"Eric was great fun. I was lost and lonely when I arrived from the village and he certainly cheered me up with a lot of juicy anecdotes about our family members. He told me that Uncle Kobby was always very fond of you."

"Eric told you that! How dare he! He was then a very naughty teenager full of mischief and Kobby banned him from his house. As regards to Mr Bandile, I have also observed his inclinations and decided to avoid being left alone with him despite his numerous attempts to corner me."

"So what happened last night when you three adults were left on your own?"

"We all talked; but Mr Bandile all the while kept staring at me. I was thoroughly embarrassed as crafty uncle Kobby looked on and pretended he did not know what was happening."

"Well, well, well! I am happy for you, Auntie. Mr Bandile is quite handsome, pleasant and rich by my humble guess and I hope your relationship turns romantic one day, maybe soon; after all we still have two days to go on this gorgeous boat."

"Robyn you are indeed a romantic dreamer and no big deal that my naughty nephew took advantage of you."

Robyn protested strongly. "He did not! It was mutual, I was equally guilty, I led him on enthusiastically and now totally regret that I did so."

"You have then learned that playboys must not be encouraged, why are you then promoting Mr Bandile who obviously is a master playboy? That is hypocrisy."

"No," said Robyn. "The two situations are totally different; in our case I was a minor and we were close relatives and by definition incestuous and a taboo, but in your case, you are both mature responsible unrelated adults unless you know something which I do not know."

"You have already started arguing like a lawyer. It must be in your blood bequeathed to you from your grandfather Stonewall and Uncle James."

"Oh! auntie that is a compliment, thank you very much."

Robyn got out of the chair, strolled to her aunt and embraced her tenderly.

The long day was devoid of actual travelling because the *M.V. Accra* was at anchor. Robyn and Debbie were entirely on their own as Uncle Kobby and Mr Bandile had gone on a tour of Lagos.

The probed the inner emotions of each other using their superlative feminine intuitions to the fullest. Robyn suspected that her auntie was still having an affair with Uncle Kobby, but she had no proof. She did her best to put Aunt Debbie off guard by cleverly suggesting that Mr Bandile was head over heels in love and perhaps the feeling was mutual and the two were together that first night. Robyn was trying to get Debbie off guard to say that she was rather with Uncle Kobby and not with the stranger Bandile. Debbie, being equally clever, recognised Robyn's machinations and said nothing to divulge the truth. Robyn was forced to conclude that her suspicions were spurious and what Eric had told her about Kobby and Aunt Debbie was false. Nevertheless, she resolved to remain vigilant during the rest of the journey in order not to miss tell-tale happenings. Debbie on the other hand had discerned from their long conversation sometimes bordering on a battle of wits that Robyn knew too much and was trying hard to substantiate a suspicion of a love affair between Kobby and her good self. She therefore resolved to be careful during the rest of the voyage in order to deny her precocious niece the proof she was insolently pursuing.

The remaining two days of the voyage was thus reduced to a silent contest between Robyn and her aunt. Both played the game so well that neither Kobby nor Bandile got wind of it. For the rest of the journey the two ladies remained glued to each other and the gentlemen did not get a moment with either of them one on one. They only met at table where the conversation was always lively and friendly. The strange episode was interpreted by eager on lookers thus: 'Debbie was being overzealous in her role as chaperon, while on the other hand Robyn was depressed and therefore needed the constant companionship of her elderly aunt to the exclusion of all other social interactions. The final part of the voyage to Calabar started shortly after midnight when the *M.V. Accra* glided smoothly from Lagos harbour with fanfare. The party on board for the passengers continued in the bars, lounges and decks until about 2.00 am when all passengers returned to their cabins. Aunt Debbie and Robyn had earlier on craftily detached themselves from Kobby and Bandile and hurried to their cabin.

ARRIVAL AT CALABAR

The *M.V. Accra* was cruising smoothly when they woke up on the morning of 7th August at 7.30 am. The sea was calm, and breakfast at 8.30 am was a very special full English breakfast. The rest of the entire day was devoted to sailing on the high seas with neither land nor birds interrupting the seascape which the passengers therefore enjoyed to the fullest. Lunch at 1.00 pm was routine, but they were given notice that dinner was going to be a special for obvious reasons.

The last dinner on the southbound voyage was always a special occasion, and the current one turned out to be no exception. They were treated to a multi-course dinner with the choicest of wines, brandies, liqueurs plus a wide assortment of cakes and puddings almost mimicking Christmas time. There was also dance music and the atmosphere was charged with hilarious holiday enjoyment. Activities came to a formal end at midnight and they all went to bed soon after for a well-earned rest in order to wake up fully re-invigorated for the anticipated morning disembarkation.

On waking up in the morning of Friday 8th August they observed that the ship was cruising gently north eastwards in a broad estuary bordered on both sides by mountainous terrain covered by a picturesque canopy of the lush green vegetation of the tropical rain forest. The boats' sirens hooted to signal that arrival and anchoring were imminent; soon the scene changed with the appearance of tall cranes making them aware that they were about to berth at the inland port of Calabar. Calabar was the capital of the British Colonial Administration of Southern Nigeria and was also a frontier town because across the river was Cameroun, which was a German colony, explaining why there were so many Germans on the boat. In the eyes of the uninitiated African native all white Europeans be they English, German, French or other looked and dressed in the same manner and showed similar unfriendly attitudes and disdain to the black natives. The only differences noticed only by the educated or urbanized blacks were their languages and the fact that they hardly ever socialized and were obviously at loggerheads with each other, sometimes feuding openly to the brink of war despite the fact their Royal families were closely related to each other by inter-marriage.

Disembarkation at Calabar, a natural deep harbour was brisk. Workers were busy off-loading large packages and equipment with cranes at one end of the ship while at the other end were the numerous passengers at the end of their voyage but still with long land treks ahead of them before they reached their final destinations all over Nigeria and Cameroun. The small Gold Coast group consisting of Debbie and Robyn looked immaculate in their well-tailored native blouses and long skirts while their male companion Kobby was wearing one of his light-weight beige suits imported from Regent Street in London. As soon they came down the gangway of the ship and entered the large disembarkation hall on land, they spotted a tall, elegant woman standing out of the crowd conspicuously because of her Accra styled outfit. They knew at once that she was their hostess.

They rushed towards her. At that very moment she also spotted them and they approached each other, almost rudely pushing the crowds out of their way. Mrs Bernadette Kaiser, as Robyn's aunt was officially known, was followed by a group of household servants who had come to assist her to welcome her guests. Aunt Bernadette embraced her niece Robyn warmly and exclaimed, "Atuuu!"

She repeated same for her sister-in-law Debbie whom she recalled meeting once several years ago when they were both very young and slim. Uncle Kobby was greeted with a simple handshake as the maximum local custom allowed under the circumstances. Kobby was the first to speak as the ladies were utterly dumbfounded with over excitement.

"Dear Mrs Kaiser, we are indeed happy to be here. We spotted you from a great distance though we have hardly met before nor even seen your recent photograph. You however shone like a beacon in the crowd and have made us proud."

Mrs Kaiser thanked him for the compliment and added,

"You also stood out in your splendid outfits and as soon as we spotted you, I announced to all and sundry, 'Behold my kinsmen and guest'. I must confess that whenever I meet my kinsmen, I become overwhelmed with homesickness and nostalgia so much so that I wonder what I am doing here among strangers. Perhaps when we arrive at my home in a couple of hours you will sympathise with me and appreciate what really is keeping me here."

The two groups walked to a quiet corner of the hall and exchanged more pleasantries. Mrs Kaiser once more gave Robyn a long hug, stepped back and looked at her from head to toe and said, "You are very good looking! Please pardon my under-statement for the truth is that you are very beautiful, indeed even more beautiful than your mother despite the close resemblance."

Uncle Kobby was quick to remark that some of Robyn's beauty derived from Quintin-Taki genes.

"That may well be, which proves that Robyn inherited a double dose of beauty."

The welcoming activities recounted above took about 30 minutes which allowed the servants enough time to identify and assemble the luggage of the disembarking ladies. As soon as the luggage was cleared by the customs officials, they all walked through immigration without any checks as they were British Colonials. Meanwhile the Cameroonians, the Germans and French were subjected to strict immigration procedures before they were allowed to enter Calabar, the capital of British Southern Nigeria.

The luggage was loaded on to the cargo cart pulled by two strong horses. The servants joined the driver in the open cabin behind the horses which he controlled skilfully with the reins and a long whip. Mrs Kaiser and her important visitors were led to a magnificent vehicle pulled by well-groomed horses driven by a professional uniformed driver. Soon they were on their way navigating through the narrow crowded noisy streets of Calabar. Suddenly all was quiet and they were out of town galloping at moderate speed along a narrow brown dusty road deep in the jungle. The rough sounds of wheels and rhythmic clatter of hoofs of horses on the hard dusty road did not hamper their conversation, which on the contrary became rather charged and animated because Mrs Kaiser, a proper talkative, was excited by these truly colourful visitors from her native Gold Coast. Crowded in the small cosy vehicle, and thoroughly pre-occupied with the jungle greenery and animated conversation, time literally flew and they were amazed when they were informed by the efficient driver that they had been on the road for two hours and that they were ten minutes from home.

The ride became smoother and that was the signal that they were in the estate. The gates of the magnificent Kaiser mansion came into view at the far end of the absolutely straight tree-lined drive: all the visitors gasped for breath when they finally reached the threshold of Robyn's new abode for the next several years. They were led by Mrs Kaiser first to a high-ceilinged porch and then through tall double doors with golden knobs to enter a magnificent cathedral-like foyer furnished tastefully with colourful printed curtains and several beautiful sofas against the walls. The foyer opened up into the main lounge which was exquisitely furnished in typical German-Swiss fashion. The beautiful chairs in the lounge were so irresistibly inviting that all the visitors experienced a compulsion to sit in them. It was 11.30 in the morning, still quite cool indoors in this forest zone. Since it was not yet lunch time their well-mannered hostess offered them tea or lemonade with biscuits and cakes. They all opted for tea. In exactly five minutes piping hot Swiss tea was served using beautiful tea pots, cups and saucers of the finest Chinese craftsmanship. Home-baked cakes and tasty imported biscuits were also served. The atmosphere was pleasant, the cakes were tasty and the Swiss tea invigorating enough to stimulate conversation. Uncle Kobby was quick to take advantage of the situation by throwing an obvious question to the good-natured Mrs Kaiser.

"By the way Mrs. Kaiser how did you come by such a beautiful mansion deep in the forest so far away from the Gold Coast?"

"Well, it is rather a long story. My late husband was Swiss but acquired British citizenship through prolonged stay in northern London where he ran a very famous hotel. He ran into trouble when he was suspected of being a German spy, which he was not. He was tried and 'banished to the overseas colonies' specifically to Australia. Due to a peculiar reason, he opted for Gold Coast Colony to work as manager of a family oil palm plantation on which my parents lived and worked. There we fell in love and got married even ahead of my older sister's – Robyn's late mother-- marriage to Mr Jeff Quinton-Taki. After our marriage, my husband felt uncomfortable on the farm for several reasons and suggested that we move far away in order to preserve the marriage. As soon as I agreed he started searching in earnest. He found and bought this place from an ageing Swiss master baker who wished to retire to his chalet on Lake Geneva. We came here fifteen years ago, and the hard work we put in yielded fruits. Unfortunately, my husband died two years ago when our bakery business was at its peak and we were the only producers of European bread and pastries in this part of the world. One year before he died, we had dispatched our sixteen-year-old son to London to complete his matriculation and go to University to study science and medicine. The funds required for education in London are prohibitive, however since it was my husband's principal wish, I am fully committed to see it through hence the enthusiasm to continue the business. I am talking too much history; I prefer the exciting current affairs thrust upon us."

Looking directly into the eyes of her beautiful niece she said,

"Well, Robyn, welcome to your new home! I really feel good because at last I have a living in relative and companion who by all standards is beautiful, intelligent and above all friendly. Now my dutiful in-laws uncle Kobby and sister Debbie, you are also welcome to my humble abode."

EPILOGUE

The first part of this multi-part saga started with the dramatic first encounter of the principal characters Eric and Robyn in the mansion of Lawyer James Quinton-Taki at mid-morning on that fateful day in the year of our Lord 1900. The drama unfolded with turbulent scenes of secret interactions and seductions which exploded into the scandalous and incestuous union between first cousins culminating in a pregnancy and birth of a baby girl named Martha. There followed a crisis which nearly broke up the marriage of young Eric Wuta. The skilful intervention of Eric's extended family led by Lawyer James Quinton-Taki, Eric's uncle and head of the Quinton-Taki family and the magnanimity of Eric's wife and her family resulted in a reconciliation conditional on forced separation, if necessary, of the incestuous couple to render it impossible for them to see each other for a very long time. The first volume of this novel thus ends here with the perfect execution of the separation worked out by James Q-T who planned the voyage from Accra to Calabar.

www.ingramcontent.com/pod-product-compliance
Ingram Content Group UK Ltd.
Pitfield, Milton Keynes, MK11 3LW, UK
UKHW040006200726
13854UKWH00001B/67

9 789988 902339